From Italy with Love

Other Large Print Books
in this series:

From Italy With Love, Book One
    by Gail Gaymer and DiAnne Mills

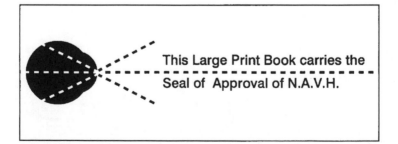

This Large Print Book carries the
Seal of Approval of N.A.V.H.

Book Two

From Italy with Love

Motivated by Letters, Two Women Travel to Italian Cities and Find Love

Melanie Panagiotopoulos
Lois Richer

Thorndike Press • Waterville, Maine

Published in 2005 by arrangement with
Barbour Publishing, Inc.

Thorndike Press® Large Print Christian Fiction.

The tree indicium is a trademark of Thorndike Press.

The text of this Large Print edition is unabridged.
Other aspects of the book may vary from the original edition.

Set in 16 pt. Plantin by Liana M. Walker.

Printed in the United States on permanent paper.

Library of Congress Cataloging-in-Publication Data

Panagiotopoulos, Melanie.
   [To Florence with love]
   From Italy with love : To Florence with love; and,
   Roman holiday.
     p. cm. — (Thorndike Press large print Christian fiction)
   ISBN 0-7862-7388-7 (lg. print : hc : alk. paper)
   1. Motion picture actors and actresses — Fiction.
2. Grandmothers — Death — Fiction. 3. Florence (Italy)
— Fiction. 4. Rome (Italy) — Fiction. 5. Large type books.
I. Richer, Lois. Roman holiday. II. Title: Roman holiday.
III. Title. IV. Thorndike Press large print Christian fiction
series.
PS3616.A358T6 2005
  813´.6—dc22   2004029030

From Italy
with Love

As the Founder/CEO of NAVH, the only national health agency solely devoted to those who, although not totally blind, have an eye disease which could lead to serious visual impairment, I am pleased to recognize Thorndike Press★ as one of the leading publishers in the large print field.

Founded in 1954 in San Francisco to prepare large print textbooks for partially seeing children, NAVH became the pioneer and standard setting agency in the preparation of large type.

Today, those publishers who meet our standards carry the prestigious "Seal of Approval" indicating high quality large print. We are delighted that Thorndike Press is one of the publishers whose titles meet these standards. We are also pleased to recognize the significant contribution Thorndike Press is making in this important and growing field.

Lorraine H. Marchi, L.H.D.
Founder/CEO
NAVH

★ Thorndike Press encompasses the following imprints: Thorndike, Wheeler, Walker and Large Print Press.

To Florence
with Love

Melanie Panagiotopoulos

Dedication

With much love to my brothers,
Derek and Chris and their lovely families.
And with many thanks to
Christina Nevada Caughlan and
David Maria Massei,
who were friends to a stranger
when friends were needed the most.
God bless you all!

Therefore, as God's chosen people,
holy and dearly loved,
clothe yourselves with compassion,
kindness, humility, gentleness
and patience.
Bear with each other
and forgive whatever grievances
you may have against one another.
Forgive as the Lord forgave you.
And over all these virtues put on love,
which binds them all together
in perfect unity.
COLOSSIANS 3:12–14

Prologue

Samantha Day breezed into the marble foyer of her elegant Fifth Avenue penthouse. She deposited a Barneys New York silver-lettered black shopping bag on the hall table, while tossing her heather gray cashmere sweater across the shoulder of the human-sized reproduction of Michelangelo's statue of David. She was probably one of the few people in the world who could buy a designer evening gown that cost more than most people made in a month of working and walk out of the store with it casually dropped into a bag without there being even the hint of a smile on her lips. But smiling was not something Samantha Day did often.

"Ms. Day." Her housekeeper addressed her, and while carefully removing the Oscar de la Renta sweater from the statue, the small woman dressed in an immaculate housekeeper's uniform motioned toward the library with its tastefully decorated, classical motif. "Several letters arrived for you this morning. One came by special delivery from Texas."

"Texas?" Samantha turned and cast her famous eyes, known most for their natural color, an amazing design of green encircled by two aquamarine rings, in the direction of her housekeeper. Whenever she played a psychopathic killer or a bitter housewife wanting to get even with her cheating husband or any other similar role, her eyes had been written up in movie reviews as being creepy, chilling, scary. They looked a bit that way now as she regarded her housekeeper.

"Yes, Ma'am." The woman nearly stammered, and with a regal nod of her head and its expertly dyed, blond hair, Samantha dismissed the older woman. Samantha coolly regarded her housekeeper as she all but scurried down the marble hall and out of sight. She hated the way the woman seemed almost afraid of her. But that was the problem with the roles she had played. Too many people confused who she really was with the acts she performed.

Sighing, she turned toward the letter that sat propped and waiting against the lamp on her glass-topped pediment desk. Her two-inch Manolo Blahnik heels, which gave her a height of five feet eleven inches, clicked across the marble floor toward it.

Reaching down, she picked up the envelope.

For just a moment, as she regarded the strong and handsome penmanship belonging to the man who had raised her — her maternal grandfather, she felt a pang of guilt, of remorse even, for her actions or rather, lack thereof, toward him during the last ten years. But she knew very well that he disapproved of both her lifestyle and her work. A slight grimace crossed the fine line of her mouth. To be one of the most highly paid movie stars in Hollywood and a Golden Globe recipient were not considered great accomplishments by her grandfather.

She stared at the name on the address.

Samantha Day.

The fact that he called her Samantha Day and not by her actual name of Florence Celini was something she often wondered about. It was true that everyone in the world knew her as Samantha Day. But it kind of confused her that her grandfather called her by that stage name, too. She had never requested he do so. If he had been a vindictive person, she might have understood his not addressing her by her actual name. She had left his home a decade earlier — after having lived with him for the same amount of time — and had never returned. But she knew that that couldn't be the reason. Her grandfather didn't have a spiteful bone in all of his six feet four inches of body.

Kicking off her shoes, she reached for the ivory and gold letter opener the director of her last film had brought back to her from Greece and neatly sliced open the sealed manila envelope.

Two pieces of mail slid from it. A loose, folded piece of binder paper and a sealed envelope made of quality stationery.

She reached first for the binder paper. She was certain that it would contain a short note from her grandfather. A high-school science teacher, he always had an abundant supply of notebook paper on hand.

Dear Samantha,
    This just arrived for you.
    I think that it might be important so I'm sending it on to you by special post.
                        All my love and prayers,
                        Grandpop

P.S. Please let me know if you need anything, anything at all.

That familiar pang that she was neglecting her grandfather — the man she had affectionately called "Grandpop" when growing up and who she still thought of in that way — went through her like a flash. But, as is the nature of a flash, it disappeared just as quickly.

Sighing, she reached for the envelope, the reason for her grandfather sending this letter by special courier.

She turned it over, and as she did, the gasp that would have been recognized by moviegoers around the world came from between her lips.

Not only was it addressed to her grandfather's address in Texas, which was the only one the sender of this letter could possibly have had, but also, it was addressed to Florence Celini, the name that was to be found on her birth certificate.

And it was from Italy.

A letter from Italy . . .

And Samantha knew then that she had been expecting this letter — forever.

She looked carefully at the return address and a frown, the world-famous one people paid big dollars to see on screen, marred the perfect smoothness of her high forehead.

The name she had expected to see on it,

that of her paternal grandfather, Lorenzo Celini, wasn't there. Rather the name of some unknown lawyer, Domenico Ferretti, and his law firm, was professionally and impersonally emblazoned across the upper left corner of the expensive envelope.

And that could mean only one thing.

Samantha's hand, with its long perfectly manicured and polished nails, started to quiver, which in turn made the envelope she was holding shake with a tremulous motion.

Her grandfather, her father's father, must have died.

Chapter 1

An ache that was as unexpected as it was fierce throbbed through her. She had never met her Italian grandfather — had never had any desire to do so since he had been so mean to her parents — but now, with all the longing of an actress who liked happy endings more than the sad ones for which she was always cast, she knew that she had, in a secret place deep inside her heart, dreamed of a reunion with the man who had never accepted her mother as good enough for the lineage that belonged to his son.

Up until that moment in which she held the envelope that most likely told of her paternal grandfather's death, she had acted out in her mind at least a thousand times how she would first berate him for having so wronged her parents, while holding out her own success as an example of how mistaken he had been about his son's choice of a bride. Afterward, after he spent some time begging for her forgiveness, she would have grudgingly granted him a partial pardon and they would have lived, if not *happily* ever after, at least somewhat *peacefully* ever after. . . .

But now, with a sadness that seemed to envelop her entire being, she wasn't so sure that that was what she would do if she was lucky enough to meet him. At this moment all she wished for was the opportunity to forgive him totally and completely without him even having to beg for her forgiveness. Isn't that what her parents would have done? Isn't that what she — Florence Celini — would have done before she became Samantha Day?

She had received only one other letter from Italy: a letter of condolence from her grandfather a few days after her parents had died in a small plane crash when she was seven. That was a letter she had long since thrown away.

She wished she could throw this letter away, too.

For all that he had treated her parents badly, simply for the crime of having fallen in love with one another, she didn't want to hear about him dying.

As far as she knew he and her American grandpop, the man she had disappointed when she had turned her back on most of his Christian teachings, were her only living relatives. Neither her parents, nor she, had siblings.

She looked at the name of the lawyer again.

Domenico Ferretti.

She wished that she never had to open Mr. Ferretti's letter.

But she knew that she had to. And the sooner she did so, the better.

Using the same instrument to slice open this envelope with its fine Florentine stationery as she did the manila one, she swiftly cut into the fold, segregating it, and, without hesitation, pulled the letter from its envelope and read it.

Dear Ms. Celini:

I am writing on behalf of your paternal grandfather, Lorenzo Celini, who greatly wishes that you might travel to Florence, Italy as soon as possible so that you might meet.

A gasp emanated from Samantha.

He was alive!

Her Italian grandfather was alive!

And he wanted to meet her!

Her knees went weak at the unexpected, but most welcomed, news, and feeling faint, she sank into the chair behind her as she continued reading the formal, and yet very friendly, letter.

> *He greatly regrets the years that have gone by without your having met and begs your indulgence and forgiveness.*
> *Please call this office — a collect phone call — so that arrangements can be made. Your fare, accommodations, and spending money will be taken care of while you are here.*
> *Yours very sincerely,*
> *Domenico Ferretti*

The letter slid from her fingers. Her paternal grandfather was still alive. Alive! And he wanted a reunion with her!

Like being given a second chance, she felt a sense of happiness fill her unlike anything she had felt since she had left her grandpop's home.

But, as so often happens when people make pledges when in distress, as she had done a moment earlier when she thought her paternal grandfather had died, it didn't last.

Even while still riding on a wave of delight, reality crashed down upon her, as all that made her the movie star, Samantha Day, imperiously demanded of her the *reason* why she should forgive her Italian grandfather.

He had found her mother — without even giving the woman a chance to prove herself — to be unworthy, had consequently turned his back on his only son, then on his only grandchild. What sort of man did that?

A man whose personality Samantha Day's greatly resembles, a still small voice whispered to her soul, and a shudder rippled through her slender body.

She reached down and picked up her grandpop's handwritten note. She looked at it and whispered as if to the man himself, "Why couldn't I have been more like you, Grandpop? Life would have been so much easier, simpler."

You could be, that still, small voice whispered to her again. *You can be — or act — in any way you choose. It's all about volition.*

Her left eyebrow curved upward and irony glinted in her eyes. She was an actress. Who better aware of that truth than she? She made her living — and a very good one — *acting* in different roles.

Slowly, then more quickly, a plan formed in her head. She *would* go to Italy to meet her long lost grandfather. She looked down at the name on the envelope — her name — Florence Celini.

Evidently her Italian grandfather didn't know who she was now. But that was only as she expected it to be. Practically no one knew that Samantha Day and Florence Celini were one and the same.

In her usual decisive manner, she determined to keep it that way.

She would go to Florence to meet her grandfather but she wouldn't go as Samantha Day, the movie star.

No.

She would go as Florence Celini, her parents' daughter — until it suited her to do otherwise.

Getting excited with the thought of playing *herself* in a role, she paused as it occurred to her that she didn't know *who* Florence Celini was anymore. Samantha Day — the cool, aloof, femme fatale — she knew and played perfectly. But Florence Celini, that was something entirely different.

Walking over to the picture window and its enviable view of Manhattan she contemplated who she might have been had the film star, Samantha Day, not intruded upon her life. That was a question for which she had few answers. Neither did she have a script nor a ready-made character profile on Florence Celini in which to read either. She considered that she probably would have still been working in her parents' former bookstore on Main Street in the gulf town in which her grandfather lived. Maybe she would have owned the store again by now. That had always been her dream: to buy back her parents' bookstore.

When had she forgotten that?

She shook her head. That wasn't the point right now. *Who* she would have been, was.

She looked in the direction of where her housekeeper could be heard preparing lunch. One thing was for sure; Florence Celini certainly wouldn't be a person who made others feel afraid of her. Of that she was certain.

But with her blue-green gaze scanning over the trees of Central Park she knew that she would find the answers.

She would.

Because to *play* the part of herself and to travel to Italy as Florence Celini excited her more than anything she had done in a good long time. She somehow knew that this was something she had to do before the strong personality of the movie star,

Samantha Day, totally erased that of Florence Celini.

That brought her thoughts to a screeching halt.

Is that what was happening to her? Had she lost the actual person she was behind the persona of a Hollywood movie star?

She sighed irritably and touched her blond hair.

So much more had changed about her than just the color of her hair.

She had been blond from the beginning of her career. No one — except for her grandpop, hairdresser, and agent — knew that her actual color was chestnut brown. She would start there. She would cut it, too, cut the long locks of honey blond — her showbiz trademark — that cascaded down past her shoulder blades. Chin length brown hair and a pair of studious-looking glasses in the place of her clear contact lenses would take care of a disguise. And if anyone asked what she now did she would say that she owned bookstores. It wasn't a lie. She loved bookstores and as a sort of hobby, and at the advice of her accountant who had been searching for tax breaks for her, she had invested in a chain of them. She owned seven shops now throughout the Northeast. Each personal and small, just like that one on Main Street where she had worked after high school most every day and where she had been when she had been discovered by the man who was still her agent.

She walked back to her desk and, picking up the lawyer's letter, ran her fingertips across the gold embossed name and address there.

Domenico Ferretti.

Now that was a good Italian name. She wondered what he looked like. A tall, dark, and handsome man who might be cast for the lead in a spy movie, perhaps? Would he have a strong chin, the classic Italian face that Michelangelo Buonarroti might have deemed worthy to immortalize in Carrara marble, but with the actual olive skin that was warm and smelled as good as it looked?

"Probably fat and bald with a paunch the size of a basketball," she mumbled as she reached for her phone and punched out his number.

As she listened to the beeps and hums of the connection going through on the phone lines, she turned her head and looked over her shoulder toward the Manhattan skyline. It was magnificent, vibrant. It was . . . New York.

And a smile — one almost of contentment — curved her perfect lips. New York in its entire twenty-first century splendor was beautiful — magnificent even. But she *was* looking forward to exchanging it for the Renaissance refinement of Brunelleschi's dome, Giotto's bell tower, and the medieval store-lined Ponte Vecchio — Old Bridge — in the river valley of the Arno. Florence was not only home to half her ancestors, but she somehow felt that it was a place for her future, too. A pilgrimage of sorts to discover whom Florence Celini might still be.

The call went through, and upon identifying herself to a secretary, Florence only had to wait a moment before a strong male voice broke through the line, startling her from her reverie.

"Good day, Ms. Celini. I'm Domenico Ferretti. I'm so happy that you called." The voice did not sound at all as if its owner possessed a fat tummy. In fact, if his voice was anything to go by, it sounded as if he was not only a perfect specimen of a classically handsome Italian — tall, dark, and extremely handsome — but also one with an Oxford flare. A distinctive British accent, spiced by an Italian upbringing, gave his voice a sonance that was as charming as it was unique. Being a voice person, Florence decided that this man's definitely had merit.

"I only just received your letter." She paused. "It came as a bit of a shock."

"As I wrote to you, your *nonno* — grandfather — greatly wishes to meet you." He was articulate and firm without being haughty. "He deeply regrets the years that have passed without him acting in the role of your grandfather."

Acting? She frowned. *Did* her grandfather and his lawyer, Domenico Ferretti, know something about her professional life. She would continue as if they didn't until she knew for sure. "I have another grandfather, one who has been very kind to me." *Much more so than I deserve,* that little voice of conscience whispered to her even as her antagonistic words came out.

"I'm glad to hear it. I know your *nonno* will be, too." He paused, then, when she remained silent, he asked, "When will you be able to travel to Florence?"

"I don't believe that I've said that I'm able to come." She didn't know what made her say that. Maybe the way he called her paternal grandfather *nonno?* Although she knew it was the Italian word for grandfather, it somehow seemed too familiar, too nice, too caring on the part of a man who had shown none of those characteristics. And in spite of her determination to travel to Italy, it rubbed her the wrong way.

"I hope that you are able to do so," Domenico Ferretti replied smoothly, totally unperturbed by her stand.

She remained silent. It was obviously his job to get her to travel to Florence. Samantha Day wouldn't make it easy for him.

"If getting leave from your work is the problem, I would be happy to talk to your employer." His voice seemed to fade a bit so she knew that he had taken his mouth away from the phone and was looking at something. "Caller ID indicates that you're at a number in New York City. Manhattan," he qualified. "Is that where you're living now?"

That answered her question about whether they knew of her as Samantha Day, the actress. If they had he wouldn't have needed Caller ID to tell him where she was calling from or, for that matter, he wouldn't have sent the letter to her grandpop's address. "I'm impressed, Signor Ferretti." She couldn't see him of course, but she was almost certain from the length of the pause that a smile had flickered across his lips. In the true spirit of her thespian soul she couldn't help musing what those lips looked like.

"The wonders of the computer age." *Yes, there was definitely a smile in his voice.* "The Medicis would have loved it."

She knew that he referred to the banking family of the fifteenth century that had been one of the major monetary influences responsible for the flowering of the intellectual and artistic life for which Florence was still famous. Her gaze went to the M section of her library. She had numerous books about the Medicis. "Their banks throughout Europe probably never would have run into mismanagement problems if Cosimo dé Medici or his progeny had had a Bill Gates among the contingent of brains that so added to the world during that time."

"Your knowledge of Florence's history impresses me."

She remained quiet. It was something she had learned to do long ago when she wanted to unsettle someone. But Domenico Ferretti was not the unsettling kind.

"Then again, maybe not," he continued, not seeming to find anything awkward in the pause, as she had intended. "You *are* half Florentine, after all."

"Half Italian," she corrected him.

He laughed. Not chuckled, but laughed. A deep robust sound that came through the wires, making her feel just as disturbed as a man coming through her sixth floor library window would. It was an intrusion. No one had laughed at her . . . not to her face anyway . . . ever. "You're right, of course. A true Florentine would never make such a correction."

She ran her hand across the cool glass of her desk, trying to ward off the uneasy feeling that he had just turned her words back upon her. This time she remained quiet for want of what to say; a very unusual occurrence for her. She was the queen of comebacks.

"I do hope you are able to come to Firenze — Florence — soon. Your *nonno* really does want to meet you."

She decided then that not only she, but Hollywood, too, would love the way Domenico Ferretti enunciated his words. He had a persuasive voice, but at the same time a calming one, one that seemed to caress her soul and make her feel as if he spoke the truth, made her feel that her *nonno* really did want to meet her. But hadn't Tom Knight — the man she had almost married thirteen months ago — made her feel that way, too? And that relationship had turned out disastrously. She had been dating Tom for over a year and never, not once in that entire time, did she suspect that he had only been using her to further his own acting career. Not until she had overheard him talking to his agent. . . .

She had thought Tom to be her "knight in shining armor," come to save her from the fake world with which she had become an integral part, a major cog, actually. But he hadn't been her knight at all. Only a hanger-on and one of the worst kinds, one who had hung onto her heart and then tossed it away without a care.

"Miss Celini?"

With a decisive flick of her wrist, she tossed the blond locks that had fallen over her shoulder back behind her and, with a no-nonsense tone, answered the man with the intriguing voice. "Yes, Mr. Ferretti. I'll be able to come toward the beginning of next week. Monday or Tuesday would be fine." That would give her time to dye her hair back to its original chestnut brown, have it cut, buy a wardrobe Florence Celini — the bookstore owner — might wear, and take care of any other loose ends. She had a month before she started shooting her next film. The timing was perfect. Her grandpop would have said it was God's timing.

"Wonderful," Domenico Ferretti returned and Samantha couldn't help but feel as if her decision really did make him happy. It made something resembling the start of a smile touch upon her lips. "I'll ask my secretary to make all the travel arrangements and we'll get back to you in a couple of hours with them, if that is agreeable with you."

"That would be fine."

"Your *nonno* really is anxious to meet you, Signorina Celini." He paused, as if seeming to choose his next words with care. "He has many regrets. His treatment toward you is one of his greatest."

The lump that formed in her throat caught her off guard. Was she to finally act a part that had a happy ending? She shook her head. She couldn't let herself go soft. That would only lead to disappointment. And besides, her main reason for traveling to Italy wasn't to assuage an old man's conscience, but rather to give herself both the chance and the anonymity to discover who Florence Celini was, once again. She swallowed the lump and returned, "My, and it only took him twenty-seven years to come to that conclusion?"

"Don't be too hard on him, Miss Celini. He's an old man. And to forgive is easier than to hold on to anger and bitterness. Particularly since your *nonno* is *requesting* your forgiveness."

Blood rushed to Samantha's face as both the deep-seated anger and bitterness Domenico Ferretti referred to filled her. Even though she heard a caring quality in his tone, his words made her mad. *How dare the man preach to me!* "Thank you, Counselor. I'm sure your clients have to pay big money for that advice."

"No, Miss Celini," he spoke softly. "They only have to go to one of the many churches Florence has to offer to the people of the world to learn that."

Zap! Conviction like a burning fire spread through her at his words. They were exactly the ones she might have expected her grandpop to offer, were in fact, one of the reasons she had stayed away from her grandpop for so many years. And the real reason why she hadn't bought her parents' former bookstore located in the same town as Grandpop. She would have had to go there more often, had she owned it.

"My office will get back to you as soon

as we can with the travel arrangements. Arrivederci," he said, and the line went dead.

Florence stood for a moment without moving. When she finally placed the phone in its cradle, her mouth quirked in a dry line. For some reason she was quite certain that Florence Celini — as opposed to Samantha Day — would probably agree with Domenico Ferretti that to forgive is better than to hold on to anger and bitterness. But how could she be sure?

How?

And other than being her paternal grandfather's lawyer, who was Domenico Ferretti?

Two questions for which she was anxious to find the answers.

Chapter 2

Domenico hung up the phone and, placing his elbows on his hand-carved mahogany desk, cupped his chin between the palms of his hands. His gaze sought the golden Tuscan countryside on the opposite side of the Fiume Arno — Arno River — outside the window directly in front of him.

It was a graceful land. The lilt of the green and rolling hillsides, which hid the *pietra forté* — strong stones — of the earth that had built Firenze and was one of the agents that lent the city its famous golden color, was only enhanced by the deep masculine green of the reaching, soldier-like cypress trees and that of the soft and feminine silver-green olive trees that danced in the wind like a troop of ballerinas. Stone villas and domes of churches with their campaniles dotted the land but not in an intrusive way. The builders of Tuscany had been one with the earth around them and hadn't invaded the space as people so often do when they move in upon it, but rather had joined with it, a perfect marriage. Domenico thought that, other than the architectural wonders and magnificent artworks his city possessed, it was that harmony of the surrounding countryside that people from around the world sought when they traveled to the "city of the red lily," his home.

A deep sigh rumbled from his chest.

He only hoped that its charm might work its magic on his friend and client's granddaughter, Florence Celini. From their brief conversation, Domenico had decided that Florence Celini was one tough woman.

A smile edged his mouth. She kind of reminded him of how her *nonno*, his friend Lorenzo, used to be. Bitter, haughty, moody, difficult — all in all, not a very pleasant person to be around.

But the old man had changed: A true testament to the power of God's grace. Domenico hoped that that same grace might fill Lorenzo's granddaughter's heart and that she might soften toward Lorenzo. Because as things stood now, Domenico was certain that she harbored a great deal of enmity toward her *nonno*. And he didn't want her to hurt the old chap.

A year ago, their meanness would have been perfectly matched.

But not now. Lorenzo was finally a man after God's own heart, and he was using the time remaining him on earth to try and undo some of the harm he had done to his fellow humans during the seventy-nine years he had lived. And his granddaughter was high on his list of wrongs to make right.

"Dear Lord, please bring peace to Lorenzo's granddaughter, Florence. Your peace." Domenico whispered out his plea to the God he had loved, known, and trusted since he was a young boy. "And please bring about a reunion between grandfather and granddaughter that will make all the angels in your heaven sing."

Swiveling his chair around, Domenico looked at the view that he possessed from the window behind his desk. The dome of the *Duomo* — Cathedral — of Santa Maria del Fiore, seemed to float above the rooftops of Firenze. It was as inspiring to Domenico as the green earth he gazed at from his front window but in a different way. That beautiful structure — the fourth largest cathedral in the world — had been built in honor of the God who had been worshipped on this land from the middle of the third century when Greco-Syriac merchants had brought Christianity to

Roman Florentia — the name by which Florence had then been known.

He suspected that for Florence Celini to find the truth it represented and proclaimed was probably the only way she would ever be able to "clothe" herself with the compassion, kindness, humility, gentleness, and patience that she would need in order to forgive the grievance — one Domenico could well understand — that she harbored against her *nonno*. To have ignored his only grandchild — and an orphaned one at that — was an unnatural response from a grandparent. But Lorenzo *had* changed.

A frown sliced across his face. Unlike Giovanna the previous year.

Giovanna Lazzareschi.

Domenico glanced at the calendar. Today would have been their first year wedding anniversary *if* she hadn't taken his heart, chewed it up, then spat it out again.

He sighed. To learn that the woman he had loved had been nothing more than a conniving fortune hunter hadn't been easy. But he had thanked God every single day since that he had found out that her love for him had all been an act to get what she had really been after in their relationship — his social standing and wealth —

before they had married. He — both of them, so he'd thought — had wanted a child quickly. A shudder ripped through him and, closing his eyes, Domenico whispered out, "Thank you, Lord. Thank you for protecting me from such a wife . . . and the child we might have had from such a mother."

Reaching for his phone in order to instruct his secretary to make travel arrangements for Florence Celini, he paused before lifting it to add, "And please, Lord, protect Lorenzo from his granddaughter. Don't let her hurt him. Please fill her heart with Your love and Your grace. In Jesus' name I pray."

Florence picked up her grandpop's handwritten note once again. She ran her fingertips over the strong letters, and as she did, she could just imagine him sitting at his desk by the window — with the weeping willows waving so softly in the breeze outside it — writing to her. Walking over to the white leather sofa she sat, but she didn't look out at the million-dollar view of Central Park or at Manhattan itself, but rather, she looked within herself.

Who would Florence Celini be now if the professional life of Samantha Day hadn't become so all-consuming, so all-demanding? What would she believe? Where would she be living now? How would she act on this trip to Florence — the city of her ancestors for which she had been named — to meet her long-estranged grandfather?

She sighed, that sound for which Samantha Day was so famous, a sound that really belonged to Florence Celini. She really had no idea who she would have been.

But what had the lawyer with that deep and caring voice said?

" 'To forgive is easier than to hold on to anger and bitterness. Particularly since your *nonno* is requesting your forgiveness,' " she repeated his words, but this time, using all her acting skills, she clamped down on the anger that wanted to erupt within the short-tempered person Samantha Day was. Closing her eyes she leaned her head back against the sofa and allowed his words to wash through her brain, to soak it. She had thought even when he had spoken them that they were words her grandpop would have said. But thinking back, way back into the fabric of her mind, she was almost certain that her mother and father would have said the same thing and, even more, that her parents would have accepted the olive branch that her Italian grandfather was extending. Accepted it with open arms.

Her mother and father . . .

She was sure that they would have been disappointed in the woman she had grown into. Not because she had chosen a career in acting, as she knew her grandpop was, but rather because she hadn't grown up to be the woman of faith that they would have wanted her to be.

"Woman of faith." Her eyes popped open and she jumped up. "Of course," she said, as she paced in front of the window. "Florence Celini, without the star, Samantha Day's intrusion, would have been a *woman of faith*." She clicked her fingers together like she always did when inspired. "A good Christian woman just like . . . her parents had been . . . who always went to church and . . . tried to help others as much as possible . . . and . . . who read . . . the Bible. . . ."

"Bible!" As if a light had been flicked on within her, her whole face lit up. Skipping over to the B section of her extensive personal library she immediately spied the white bound volume with the words *Holy Bible* emblazoned across its spine. Since it

41

was near the top of the case, she had to stand on her tiptoes to pull it down. She held it before her and blew on its upper edge. When no particles of dust flew free, a pang of guilt that it was dirt free only because of the thorough cleaning it received from her housekeeper, and not because of use, gave her that same burning feeling of conviction that she had felt when Domenico Ferretti had said that people only have to go into one of his city's churches to learn about forgiveness.

Shaking her head as if to clear it, she returned to her favorite spot on her sofa by the gold-plated reading lamp. For just a moment she held the Bible that her parents had given to her when she was a young girl and just looked at it. It was as new and glossy looking as it had been the day they had presented it to her.

Her lips twisted in the direction of a smile.

She remembered that day. It had been Easter, their last Easter together. She was wearing an Easter dress of soft pastel pink with a sash of pure Chinese silk. Her shoes had been shiny new Mary Janes, white, without a single scruff mark on them yet. And she had had a hat, an Easter bonnet of the same pink as her dress with white ribbons that hung all the way down to the middle of her back.

She had been so happy then. So happy.

She shook her head. That had been then. Twenty years earlier. This was now. Twenty years later. And what she had to do at this moment was to find out how Florence Celini might act on this trip to Italy.

She took a deep breath, and for the first time in more years than she could remember, she opened the Bible. She flipped to the first page, then to the second; but while turning to the next, something strange happened. The pages seemed to be stuck together.

Frowning she slid her long nail along the edge of the page. The second and third pages were definitely adhering, almost as if they had been glued together.

"Not even the publishers of Bibles can do a good job these days," she grumbled. But when she carefully pried the pages apart and a long inscription — a letter actually — greeted her eyes, she gasped.

Her gaze flew to the signature.

Both her parents had signed!

Florence blinked. Then she blinked again. She thought she was dreaming.

But she wasn't. Softly, lovingly she ran her fingertips over the words her mother's neat hand had penned. Feeling her hands start to shake Florence cupped them together as her gaze scanned across the words that had been written to her and placed within this book for safekeeping so that she would someday find them.

To Florence, with love . . .

It began, and with the words of love that came through time to reach Florence at this moment she most needed her parents' advice, tears washed the corners of her eyes. But it was the words at the end of the letter that most captured Florence's attention.

. . . and should a letter ever arrive for you from Italy asking you to go meet your father's father, go and do so with a gracious heart, forgiving your grandfather for the estrangement. Life is too short not to forgive, dear Daughter, and it is a part of the Christian life when requested. A person can forgive and go on with life. Without forgiveness, however, a bitter hole remains within a person's soul: A hole that grows through the years like a cancer . . .

And never forget these wonderful verses:

"Therefore, as God's chosen people, holy and dearly loved, clothe yourselves with compassion, kindness, humility, gentleness and patience. Bear with each other and forgive whatever grievances you may have against one another. Forgive as the Lord forgave you. And over all these virtues put on love, which binds them all together in perfect unity." (Colossians 3:12–14)

With all our love and hope that you should never choose to "wear" — or act at — any life other than the life of virtue so directed by God in these verses, your loving mother and father,
Mary and Cosimo Celini

"Mamma. Babbo." Florence softly spoke as if in answer to her parents. "Is that who I would have been had you not left me? A woman who lived a life of virtue who 'wore' such characteristics? Compassion. Kindness. Humility. Gentleness. Patience. Forgiveness. Love." Florence shook her head and turned eyes that looked at but didn't see the view outside the window. Although she had always acted in a moralistic way even to the extent of having turned down a part that had nudity in it, and for which the actress who had taken the role won the much-coveted Academy Award, Florence knew that practically none of those characteristics described who she, as Samantha Day, had become.

She made a disagreeable sound. "What *practically?* None of them do," she admitted to the empty room.

She wasn't compassionate . . . except toward animals. She wasn't kind. Samantha Day didn't even know the meaning of the word humility. And gentleness, patience, and forgiveness may as well have been rocks on the moon rather than characteristics she could be "wearing."

And love?

That was where she was the biggest failure of all.

She had spurned all the love her grandpop had wanted to give her for years, and as far as a personal relationship with a man was concerned, well, if she were honest with herself, she knew that Tom Knight wasn't the only one at fault the previous year. She might not have been "using" him to further her career but she had used him.

She nodded her head affirmatively. She certainly had.

He had been her "whipping boy." Whatever bothered her in her work or life or the world in general, she had taken it out on him. Samantha Day's temper on the set was as legendary as was the yelling that accompanied it. Again, if she were truthful, she knew that she was little different at home, hence the real reason her housekeeper seemed afraid of her. Not because of the roles she played. She'd always wondered why Tom had stayed with her. Because of the same morals that had kept her from taking that Oscar-winning role, he hadn't even been privy to the physical closeness most men in the world in which they worked and lived expected from their fiancées.

Yes. She had wondered until that afternoon when she'd heard him talking to his agent. . . .

She looked back down at the loving letter her parents had sent to her, one that had been safeguarded within the pages of her Bible — and meant for her to find when she finally cared enough to take the book off the shelf, open it, and read it carefully.

Then she looked over at the lawyer's letter, and that of her grandpop's, lying on her desk.

"An afternoon for letters," she murmured but, sighing softly, continued with, "But nice ones." Letters that she felt might just change her life.

She ran her hand over the Bible. Her grandpop had always called the Bible *Letters from God*.

She smiled, a real smile.

The Bible was another letter and one she felt might somehow show her how to act as Florence Celini. And even, she considered as she flipped to Colossians so that she could find the verses her parents had written to her, how to live that life, too.

Normally Domenico let his secretary take care of calling clients about something as mundane as travel information. But because of her latent anger and antagonism, he felt that it was important that he call Florence Celini personally. He was taken aback when the phone was answered on the first ring.

"Pronto." The friendly Italian salutation surprised him even more.

"Miss Celini?"

"That would be me."

He frowned. She was so chipper sounding, so different from the heavy

48

haughtiness of before. "Domenico Ferretti here."

"Of course. I've been waiting for your call."

He hadn't thought she was the type to sit by the phone waiting for a phone call. But he accepted the friendly atmosphere with a grateful heart and was glad, too, that he'd returned the call himself. "That's good to hear."

"When can I expect to be landing at Amerigo Vespucci Airport?"

He frowned. "You know the name of Florence's airport?"

"I've been doing some reading."

From the complete turnabout in her tone, it sounded as if she had been doing more than just the normal tourist reading, though. Would it be too much to hope that she had maybe been reading her Bible, maybe praying, too? According to information Lorenzo had given to him when they talked an hour earlier, the grandfather who had raised her was supposed to be a very strong Christian, as her parents had been. So it was possible. She just seemed so different from before. Gone was the haughty autocrat that had him concerned, and in her place seemed to be a very nice young woman. For the first time, Domenico wondered if she was married.

"I neglected to ask you before. But if there is someone special that you would like to have travel with you, his expenses will be taken care of, as well." There. That would take care of both asking if she was married and finding out if she had a boyfriend with whom she was particularly close.

"No, there's no one. I'll be traveling alone."

Domenico couldn't help how much that information pleased him. "How does arriving here at three o'clock Monday afternoon sound?"

"Wonderful. I'm looking forward to it."

Domenico blinked. *Wonderful? Looking forward to it?*

Either the woman was schizophrenic, or his prayers — and those of Lorenzo's — had done some good. She was acting totally different from before. Not just her friendly words but the tone of her voice, the way he was sure that smiles had to be touching upon her lips in between her words.

As much as it pleased him something seemed off.

He wished that he had insisted that Lorenzo allow an investigation of her before contacting her. Or maybe the shock of his letter telling about her *nonno*'s wishes for reconciliation had thrown her before. But wouldn't the woman she seemed to be now have reacted differently? Whatever, it was too late to have her investigated. He could only trust that she was who she seemed to be.

But as he gave her her travel schedule, he knew that he would watch her carefully. Very carefully. He didn't want Lorenzo hurt.

"Do you have any other questions?" he asked, after giving her the arrangements.

"No. I think I've got it. Thank you."

Bright and cheery sounding again. And as much as he wanted to, he didn't trust it. Something just didn't ring right to him. His experience as a lawyer had taught him to trust his first impression of people. If adverse, it would take several encounters of a changed individual for him to alter it. "If you have any other questions, please feel free to call this office. Collect."

"Thank you."

"I'm looking forward to meeting you, Signorina Celini." That was an understatement. For good or bad, the woman intrigued him. Not only was she Lorenzo's granddaughter, but also something about her had captivated him in a way a woman hadn't done since . . . Giovanna Lazzareschi.

He frowned. Should that be a warning to him? He was normally a pretty good judge of character. Only Giovanna had managed to trick him. And she had captivated him, too. Was that what this woman was doing to him, too? But Giovanna's exceptional physical beauty had been primarily behind that and the way she had of *acting* the part of loving fiancée. He had no idea what Florence Celini looked like. And still, she fascinated him. He liked that. It made him feel less superficial.

"Me, too, Signor Ferretti. Ciao!"

"Ciao," he replied but waited for her to hang up before he did. He looked at his phone and shook his head. Maybe he would have an interesting week for a change. That would be nice. He was ready for . . . something.

As his gaze scanned over the green and golden Tuscan hillsides, he only wondered if that something might be Florence Celini.

Chapter 3

As the small plane landed at Amerigo Vespucci Airport, Florence looked out over the green and golden mountains surrounding the city of her father's birth and couldn't shake the feeling of somehow having come home. Although she had never visited Firenze in person, she had always felt a connection to the renaissance city because of her father. She probably had every coffee-table book ever published on the little city in her library.

She just hadn't given any of the books more than a casual glance until . . . receiving Domenico Ferretti's letter.

That letter had set in motion such changes in her life, changes that were as unexpected as the letter itself had been.

She pushed her bluntly cut shoulder-length chestnut-brown hair behind her right ear.

And she meant much greater alterations than just the cutting and coloring of her hair, the discarding of contacts and donning of glasses, and a modification of her wardrobe from Carolina Herrera and Oscar de la Renta to Gap and J. Crew.

Her gaze sought out her flight bag beneath the seat in front of her and the Bible that was in its front flap.

Bible. She made an amazed sound.

She had never traveled with a Bible before.

But this one, the one that contained the letter from her parents, was one she knew she would never leave home without again. Even though she had started out using the verses in Colossians as a guide for the character sketch that might belong to Florence Celini, the verses were becoming much more to her. An identity — one linked to her parents — she now *chose* to wear. And not just in acting but for real. The more she "wore" the virtues, the more comfortable they became. She felt that they went a long way in describing the person she would have been had the fake world of movie stardom not changed the path of her life.

"Wearing" the virtues of compassion, kindness, humility, gentleness, and patience was turning her into a person whose company she actually enjoyed. It felt really strange not to be angry or disillusioned or moody all the time, something Samantha

Day had become without Florence's even understanding that it had happened or, even more, how.

But unusual, too, was how she had left her apartment in Manhattan unassisted, in a yellow city taxi rather than Samantha Day's normal limousine, had gone through all the check-in points at Kennedy Airport, and again at Rome's airport, had ridden on two airplanes, and hadn't been recognized by anyone. Not flight attendant, not gate agent, not fellow passenger. No one. On either continent or in the air in between them, either.

That was the first time since her acting career had exploded seven years earlier that that had happened. Normally she was inundated with well-wishers and celebrity-seekers. And although it was something she had never really minded, had even liked on most occasions, it was a heady experience being a private individual again — something she was enjoying. For the moment, anyway, it gave her the time she needed to think, really think, about whom she was and what she believed for the first time in years and without the persona of Samantha Day intruding upon her thoughts.

And as she left the airplane and boarded

the shuttle bus that was to take her to the terminal, she thought about her long-estranged grandfather — how he would act toward her, she toward him, and what he would look like — as well as the lawyer, Domenico Ferretti, who had said that he would be personally picking her up from the airport.

She was certain that that was something he normally didn't do. But as she left the bus and went through the doors of the terminal and scanned the small airport, she couldn't help but wonder again what Domenico Ferretti would look like. Would his body fit his voice? And his name? *Domenico Ferretti* had to be one of the nicer names she had ever heard.

She wouldn't mind if his body went together with his voice and name. She knew that to become acquainted with her grandfather was the reason she was in Firenze acting in the role of herself — private citizen, Florence Celini. But she couldn't help but wonder what meeting a man while in that role might be like. What sort of man would she, as plain old Florence Celini and not superstar Samantha Day, attract, and how might he treat her? One thing was certain: as Florence Celini, she could be sure no one would be after her to further their career, especially not a lawyer with a nice voice from Firenze.

"Signorina Celini." *That* voice spoke from behind her and she spun around to meet its owner. The fine specimen of man she beheld through her clear glasses robbed her of her breath.

Paunch the size of a basketball? Bald? This man didn't have an extra ounce of fat on his athletic frame, and as for baldness, her fingers itched to reach out and touch the rich forest of dark hair that was styled in a classic way around his face. He had the refined features of a man of pure Italian bloodline, and he was tall, too. Much taller than she, and at five feet nine, that was something she always noticed. Hollywood would definitely love to train its cameras on him.

She licked her lips, which had suddenly gone dry. "Signor Ferretti?"

"Yes." He held out his hand, but as his gaze scanned over her face, a look of recognition, like someone discovering a secret, came upon his face. Dread washed through her.

He knows who I am! She was certain of it. Why? Why did the one person to recognize her during the last twenty hours have to be one of the two she didn't want to know that Samantha Day, the film star, and Florence Celini, the bookstore owner, were the same person? Domenico Ferretti had intrigued her when only talking to him by telephone. Seeing him face to face made him many times more appealing. His body definitely fit his voice. And then some.

He blinked. "I'm sorry. I don't mean to stare. But you look just like —"

"I know," she cut him off. "I've been told that before." She was going to try and bluff her way out. Act as if to be told she looked like Samantha Day was a normal occurrence. It was, after all.

He looked at her curiously. "You mean by your parents? When you were little?"

"My parents?" What was he talking about?

"Is there anyone else who would know that you are the image of your *nonno?*"

Nonno! She nearly sagged in relief. He meant that she looked like her grandfather, her father's father, not like the movie star Samantha Day!

"No. I mean, yes. Yes, my parents did say that. When I was little." She motioned to her eyes, which were partially hidden behind her clear glasses. She thought it better to point out one of Samantha Day's most famous physical characteristics rather than to leave it to him to make a later comparison. The best defense being an offense, or some such thing. She'd learned that from playing numerous evil characters on the silver screen. "My father always told me that they were the same unusual color as his father's. Green with the same aquamarine rings." That was the reason, too, she hadn't bothered to get colored contacts to disguise the color of her eyes. She thought her father's father might have known that she had inherited his unusual eye coloring.

Domenico Ferretti's intelligent gaze looked past the lenses of her glasses and into them now. Deeply. She felt as if he were looking at much more than just their coloring. Trying to determine what sort of person she was, perhaps? "Yes, they are the same," he pronounced and took a step back, much as photographers do when trying to decide upon the picture they want to take. "But no. Not just your eyes. Everything. Your general look. Except for your height and gender, of course, you are the image of your *nonno*."

And as Samantha Day she had probably inherited his mean streak, too, she wanted to say, but of course, she didn't. Instead she kept to her physical appearance. "I inherited my height from my grandpop."

"Ah . . . your mother's father."

"That's right. The man who raised me. And you?" she asked, thinking it was time to turn the conversation away from her, something Samantha Day was an expert at doing.

His chin lifted a fraction of an inch in reaction to the unexpected question. "Me?"

She nodded. "Where did you get your height from?" She knew he had to know her history. She wanted to learn something about him. Actually, she wanted to learn a lot about him.

He smiled, a wide one that looked like it had laughter hiding right behind it. Real laughter, not a fake one brought forth upon the demand of a director. "My mother. She was actually taller than my father."

"Was?"

Sorrow pushed the humor out of his eyes. "I lost them both several years ago."

"I'm sorry." She tilted her head, and she couldn't have said what made her continue with, "So we're both orphans."

"Except I was blessed to be a man of thirty when my parents went to God's kingdom."

God's kingdom. Spoken just like her grandpop. That's where he'd always told her her parents had gone. It had always been something more substantial to her than when people tried to assure her with the cliché "They've gone to heaven, Dear." Even as a young girl, she had always been able to picture a place called God's kingdom. To say they were in heaven was too much like a fairy tale. It might be correct, theologically speaking, but it was too vague a place for her, unlearned about such things, to imagine. But God's kingdom, she could just see angels and believers living with God in that mighty place of joy and comfort. And no pain.

She shook her head. Reading her Bible had gotten her thinking about such things a lot during the last few days. More than she had in all the previous ten years put together. Unlike what she knew her grandpop thought, she had never renounced Christianity; she just hadn't been a practicing believer.

"You were . . . blessed," she agreed. *Blessed?* She hadn't used that word before. Not ever. But for some reason to say he was lucky just wouldn't have seemed correct.

He looked at her in a curious way, but in a manner that made her feel as if she had just passed a test. "They were great people.

And so in love with one another."

A man who came from a loving family? She hadn't met one of those . . . in years. Most all the men she had known during the last decade had come from broken homes. "Tell me, when will I meet my grandfather?"

His square jaw lifted a fraction of an inch, alerting her to something being wrong. One thing acting had done was make her very aware of nonverbal communication. "It was to have been immediately, but there's been a slight . . . complication."

She tilted her head to the side. "What sort of complication? Is he ill?" She hoped not. Although she couldn't muster up much feeling for the old man — even while acting in the role of herself and with wearing the virtues of Colossians Three — she really did want to meet him. He was the man who had fathered her beloved *babbo*, her daddy. As much as she might not like it, she existed because of him. She was a direct descendent of his.

"No, no," he was quick to assure. "Quite unexpectedly he had to go out of town for a few days."

So, that's how much he was looking forward to meeting me! Samantha Day wanted to blurt out. She pressed her lips together to keep the antagonistic response from flying out of her mouth. She *had* to let God's virtues rule her mind and not allow the jaded actress, Samantha Day, to have that place. Samantha wanted to assume the worse. But patience was a virtue she was sure she would be "wearing" had she not let Samantha Day become anything more than just her profession. And compassion, too. Two things she, as Samantha, had forgotten how to practice. She had to give Signor Ferretti the chance to explain.

"He greatly regrets it, but —"

"Seems to me, that my grandfather has a lot of regrets," she cut in, remembering the letter this man had sent to her and his writing how her grandfather had "greatly regretted the years that had gone by without them having met." She couldn't help the words from coming out, but was glad that the tone was the compassionate one Florence might use and not the haughty angry one with which Samantha would definitely speak.

"He does." Domenico Ferretti surprised her by answering in the affirmative, a direct response that didn't mince words. He took a deep breath, and looking at her squarely, his dark gaze settled on hers. She felt her heart pick up its rhythm in response. "Signorina, your *nonno* has asked me not to say too much about him to you. But as it is public knowledge, this I can say: He was for many years a very difficult man."

"The way he treated my parents tells me everything. I think he was more than just difficult."

Domenico Ferretti acknowledged the truth of that with a lift of his Ferragamo-clad shoulder. "But he has changed. Through the grace of God, he's much different from before, and he's now trying very hard to set right many of the wrongs for which he is responsible."

She tilted her head. "Sounds something like Charles Dickens's character, Ebenezer Scrooge, in *A Christmas Carol.*"

A quick smile turned Domenico Ferretti's full, but perfect lips, upward. "Yes, but without the ghosts. Unless we're talking about the Holy Ghost moving in his heart."

Again something Grandpop would say. It was amazing, but Domenico Ferretti and her grandpop were so similar. She hadn't thought anybody in the world believed as her grandpop did.

And couldn't she of all people under-stand about a person changing? Wasn't that what she was in the process of doing, herself? She had let her Hollywood personality intrude upon the woman she should have been. Had her *babbo*'s father done something similar? Had her grandfather's work, like her own, turned him into a person he didn't like? She thought it must be much more than just that, though, for him to have turned his back on his only child. Although she wanted to ask more questions, she respected the lawyer-client relationship that Domenico Ferretti was bound to follow and didn't. She would meet her grandfather when the time was right. Patience seemed to be a virtue she was learning. Samantha would have demanded more information.

"So." She smiled, but not the brilliant one movie goers around the world would recognize as belonging to Samantha Day, rather the soft one that had been curving Florence Celini's lips the last few days. "I guess I get to play tourist in your fine city until my grandfather returns." She shrugged her shoulders. "I can think of about twenty billion worse things to do."

She saw something like a mixture of relief and admiration come into his deep shiny eyes, but esteem, not over her appearance as had always been the case with

Samantha Day, rather, because of a high regard for her character. It was a heady experience and one she hadn't had in years. She knew that most considered Samantha Day spoiled, supercilious, and rather unpleasant and only had anything to do with her because her beauty sold box office tickets. A lot of tickets.

"It would be my pleasure if you would allow me to show you around."

Allow him? His pleasure? Had the man looked in the mirror recently? What mirror? He only had to notice all the admiring glances he'd been getting from the women in the terminal. She'd noticed them. Add to that a character of dignity that seemed more and more to remind her of her grandpop, and Florence thought he had to be just about perfect. Was this the type of man she as herself, as Florence, attracted? If so, then she had played the role Samantha Day for far too long.

"That would be great." *Great? It would be fantastic, wonderful, perfect!* "But do you have the time? To take off from your work, I mean?" That was something Samantha would never have asked. She would have just assumed it to be so.

His lips curved in an indulging way, and she knew that there was a lot more to this man than just being a lawyer or good looking or a man with Christian character.

Christian character? That thought brought all her others to a jarring stop. She really *was* changing. She had never thought of that as being an attribute before. For her grandpop, maybe, and her *babbo.* But not for a man her age whom she might be interested in getting to know better. *Interested?* That was an understatement. She was more attracted to this man than any other since the varsity football team's star quarterback when she was a freshman in high school.

"As unexpectedly as your *nonno* had to go out of town, I have found my calendar cleared. This next week I am your most willing guide. But how about if we get your bags now and get you settled. You must be tired." He started directing her toward the baggage claim area.

Even though she hadn't slept in a day, she wasn't sleepy at all. "Where will I be staying?" she asked, as she pointed out the two Louis Vuitton bags that belonged to her. She had thought to leave them behind and get nondesigner bags, regular ones. But even had she only been a bookstore owner she would have bought these bags. She loved them.

With a seemingly effortless movement, he removed her luggage from the conveyer belt and started walking in the direction of the exit. "Your *nonno* has an apartment in town that he thought you would enjoy for the days he's gone so that you can easily get into the city."

"That sounds great."

He turned to her and, with amusement glinting in his dark eyes, asked, "Are you always so easygoing?"

She laughed. She couldn't help it, but his question was proof that she was wearing the virtues found in Colossians, and "wearing" them well. "No. Not always." What an understatement!

As he directed her toward his Range Rover he said, "I must admit, when we talked the second time by phone, you seemed to be a different person from the first time."

"Really?" He had noticed the change and in only one conversation? But why not? She had felt the change in herself almost immediately upon making the decision to act differently by using the wise words found in the letter from her parents and the "letters from God," the Bible. Why shouldn't an observant person have noticed a change? Part of a lawyer's training was to "read" people after all.

But she didn't want to share all that had happened to her since receiving his letter — that would mean explaining about her professional life, her stage name, and her acting career — and she didn't want to do that. Not yet.

As they got into the car and he started driving off, she motioned toward the rear section that had what was obviously a dog fence separating it from the rest of the vehicle. "What type of dog do you have?"

"German shepherd," he replied, as he paid the parking ticket.

"They're beautiful dogs."

"None better than Michelangelo," he agreed, as he directed the car onto the roadway.

She laughed. "Do you think the actual man, Michelangelo, would appreciate your naming your dog after him?"

"As long as I let him sculpt my dog in marble, I doubt that he would mind."

"I don't know," she bantered back, with a challenging tilt of her chin. "He was supposed to have had a fiery temper."

A deep laughter rumbled from his chest. "He was both an artist and Italian. What else could one expect?"

"Oh, but Fra Angelico was both those,

too. And he was called Beato Angelico — Blessed Angelico — because he was so sweet natured."

He took his eyes off the roadway long enough to look at her with a quizzical frown. "You know about Fra Angelico?"

She nodded. "One of my favorite painters. Last year I sent out Christmas cards that had his painting of *The Annunciation* on them. I can't wait to see his work at the convent of San Marco's."

"We'll go there one day this week if you like. He's one of my favorites, too."

"It's a date."

He shook his head. "Who would have known?" he asked, as he switched lanes.

She looked at him and couldn't help the quizzical frown that cut across her face. "Known what?"

He took his eyes off the road long enough to glance in her direction. "That all this time Lorenzo had such a sweet and interesting granddaughter growing up in America."

Florence's eyelids rose and her lips formed a perfect O.

Sweet? Interesting? Yes, who would have known? Certainly not her. As she turned to look out the window toward the foothills of the mountains to the north of the city, she considered that the Italian air must be good for her. She slanted her eyes toward Domenico Ferretti, who was weaving his way through traffic that would have done Manhattan proud. Or maybe it was just being in the right company. This man's company. His letter had been the impetus behind her finding her parents' letter and, in turn, God's "letters" as given in the Bible. She glanced down at it still in the pocket of her flight bag. Still close to her.

The more she was with this man who had inadvertently so changed the path of her life, the easier she found it to wear the virtues of Colossians Three.

And the easier she found it to be herself — Florence Celini.

It was proving to be a much nicer way in which to live life than that of Samantha Day's.

Chapter 4

Less than half an hour later, Domenico watched her as she stood by the window in the living room of her grandfather's penthouse. She seemed to want to soak the city of her ancestors into her very pores.

Domenico thought her the most intriguing woman he had met . . . ever. Not only had her physical beauty nearly taken his breath away when he'd first beheld her, but her spirit — so sweet and calm — seemed to mesh with his, to communicate and mold together in a web he hadn't wanted to get loose of. Her body was long and graceful with gentle curves in all the right places, while her unblemished face was as creamy and smooth as a marble statue. His fingers begged to reach out and touch her cheek. But what he felt for her went beyond the physical. It went to the very center of him that seemed to know that this woman was one he could look at every day for the rest of his life; this was a woman with whom he could share a friendship, a romance, a love as great as that which his parents had been blessed to have.

She was so totally different from what he had expected. He had thought that she would be angry when she found out about her *nonno* being gone — the reason why he and Lorenzo had decided it would be best if he took off the week in order to spend time with her. But she had handled the situation with a refined decorum that was so seldom to be found in such exceptionally beautiful women. At least from those of Domenico's experience.

But best of all, she seemed guileless.

After the deception of Giovanna, that was one of the most important characteristics in a woman to Domenico. He had to know that a woman was honest and frank with him from the first. He didn't like surprises. Didn't want to ever give his heart away to a woman again only to discover afterwards that her agenda for marriage was based on different attributes from those of his own.

He wanted a woman to love. A woman to be his companion, his helper, his friend: a woman with whom he could share the joys of parenthood. A woman who would never be anything but truthful with him about what she believed, who she was, and what she felt. And visc versa.

He had acted like an adolescent — staring at her with a gapped-mouth expression — when she'd turned around in the airport, and he had gotten a real good look at her. He was only glad that he had been able to cover up his reaction by telling her that she looked like Lorenzo. She did. But that fact didn't have anything to do with making him stare at her in that star-struck fashion. Rather, it had everything to do with Cupid's arrow shooting him through his heart.

At this moment Domenico couldn't be happier that Lorenzo had had to leave town. Another case of God taking a situation that at first glance seemed all wrong but with the passing of time — and just a little bit of it — showed itself to be absolutely perfect. If Lorenzo hadn't had to go to Milan, then Domenico would not have had the chance to get to know his granddaughter personally and closely. Now he had a whole week.

A smile touched upon his lips as he watched the tall woman who so intrigued him breathe in deeply of the panoramic view of Firenze. She clasped her hands tightly together upon her chest. He knew what she was feeling.

Firenze's magic.

The magic of a city that probably had more artwork executed in honor of Jesus Christ than any other city in the world. From architecture, to paintings, to sculpture, to stained glass windows, Firenze had it all. And from the masters.

That was something everybody felt upon coming here, one of the city's innate charms and something that helped to make it one of the most romantic cities in the world. So many people fell in love after spending just a week together in Firenze.

His smile deepened. It had been long enough for his grandparents to fall in love — and they had been married for sixty years — and long enough too for his parents who had spent nearly fifty years together.

Domenico knew that a week would do for him. Do perfectly.

He was already enamored of her.

And she had used the word *blessed*, not *lucky*, when she'd agreed that to be orphaned at thirty, as he had been, and not seven, like she, was the better of the two. And she liked the work of Fra Angelico. Such little things, but things that were so important. Showed a character he liked.

A Christian character.

"I love it here," she spoke out suddenly

and swiveled away from the view. Her shiny brown hair danced around her chin like strands of pure Chinese silk. His mouth went dry. She was intoxicated by the view and seemed to glow with pleasure. He understood. He felt the same way about her. She motioned with her arm to the city. "It's like a little jewel with church domes and spires and bell towers sticking up everywhere." She looked back out. "And the color. It's golden. I mean it really is. I always thought it was the photographers' lenses that gave it that hue." She pointed down to the Arno River, which was moving right below them along its ancient course on its way to the sea. "Even the river seems golden in the afternoon sunlight."

"That's Tuscany. Only this land can take a brown, rather dirty river and turn it to gold."

She sighed. "I can't wait to go out and walk around the city."

"Whenever you want."

Whenever I want? "Now."

"Now?"

"Now!" She not only didn't want to waste a moment in seeing the city but also, as long as this man was here with her, she wanted to see it with him.

"You aren't tired from your trip across the Atlantic?"

Tired? After having spent as much as eighteen to twenty hours on movie sets in the past, to sit on a plane and fly across six time zones was easy for her. But she didn't disclose that. Since he hadn't figured out her stage persona she wanted to keep it that way. She wanted to give Florence Celini the chance to grow without the persona of Samantha Day intruding. "I'll sleep early tonight then be on Firenze's time zone." That's what she always did when she traveled far from New York. "So if you are indeed free, Signor Ferretti, I'd love to take a walk with you around your enchanting city."

He tipped his head to one side, and she was perplexed when he frowned. "I'm afraid that's impossible."

Impossible? What game was he playing? "But I thought you just said —"

"I can't walk around my city with a pretty lady by my side who calls me Signor. Now if that lady were to call me Domenico . . ."

Handsome and humorous, too. She could get used to that. "Domenico." The name rolled off her lips. "Such a nice name. Musical sounding. Is it a family name?"

She was surprised when he shook his head negatively. "Meaning 'of the Lord.' I was born on Sunday — the day of the Lord — so that's the name my parents gave to me."

"And are you? Of the Lord, I mean?" She didn't know what made her ask that. But since reading her Bible and now with looking out the window at the many churches that made up the city's distinctive skyline, it just seemed natural. And she really was interested, even though she was almost certain of the answer. He was too much like her grandpop not to be "of the Lord."

"I have been ever since I was a young boy and I started to understand the meaning behind the crucifixes that I saw hanging in the churches all over the city. With that supreme act of sacrifice, God won for me — for all of us — life everlasting. And not just that, but life as it is meant to be lived here and now, too. A life with Him in it, a part of my very own."

Yes, he believed just like Grandpop. And her parents. People from so many different backgrounds, different lands, and yet all believing the same thing. She smiled.

"That's beautiful." It really was. She knew her grandpop would have called it a testimony.

"And you?"

Fear clutched at her. She should have anticipated his question but she hadn't. She wished now that she hadn't brought the subject up. How was she to answer? *Truthfully,* that voice of conscience that she had heard more and more lately spoke to her. *Truthfully.* "I . . . I was raised a Christian, first by my parents then by my grandpop. And even though I'm a Christian — I do believe that Jesus is God's son and that He saved humankind when He hung on that cross." She paused. This was the hard part. "I must admit, however, to have lost both Him and my faith somewhere along the way."

"Firenze, with all its artwork, is definitely the place to rediscover both Him . . . and your faith." His voice was deep and gravelly. So encouraging. So masculine . . .

She smiled up at him.

He smiled down at her.

That connection she had felt even through the phone line shot between them like an electric charge.

She licked her lips as he softly continued with that voice, that beautiful voice of his.

"Maybe other than meeting your *nonno*, that's one of the reasons you had to come here. To give you the time to find the woman of faith that the girl of faith should have grown into."

She stopped breathing. How did he know? That was exactly what she felt like she was doing. What *felt?* She was doing. She started breathing again. But at his next words she again stopped.

"I prayed for you after our first conversation."

"What?" A week ago that would have offended her, affronted the cold, hard heart of the woman she had been. But not now. Now it left her almost dumbfounded. But in a way that made her feel warm and tingly all over. This man, who she hadn't even known, had been praying for her. *Praying for her.* Maybe prayers really did work. "What do you mean?"

"To be honest, after talking, I was afraid that you might come here and hurt Lorenzo — your *nonno*. And even though Lorenzo was a very" — he seemed to search around for the correct words — "shall we say, unpleasant man for most of his adult life, he has, because of the grace of God, changed. I prayed that the Lord might bring peace to your heart — His peace — just as He did to your *nonno* and that there might be a reunion between you and your *nonno* that will make all the angels in heaven sing." As silence reigned, he softly said, "I hope this doesn't offend you."

She shook her head. "To be honest, it would have before, but many things are changing in my life. And now, no, I'm not offended. Not at all. In fact," she smiled, a brilliant smile that came straight from Florence Celini's heart, "if you could help me rediscover how to pray, I would be grateful. It's something else I seemed to have lost the ability to do during the last ten years."

"I'd like that." He looked at her curiously, and his eyes narrowed a bit at their corners.

She shook her head. "What?"

"I'm sorry. But you looked so familiar to me when you smiled like that."

Her stage smile! She nearly groaned. She was almost as famous for it as she was for her sigh. But it hadn't come because the director had called for it. Rather, for the first time in years, that smile that had been written up as "brilliant, luminous, sparkling" had been a true reflection of how she was actually feeling.

"You said I look like my grandfather," she reminded him, hoping that would be enough. She wasn't ready to tell him about Samantha Day. Not yet. Not until she was better acquainted with Florence Celini.

"I don't know." She could tell from the way he looked at her with his intelligent eyes narrowed at their corners that he wasn't entirely convinced that that was it. She remained quiet and was glad she did when he shook his head as if to clear it from all the possibilities that were running through his mind. He finally said, "You're right, of course, that must be it."

"Now, shall we go see the city?" She was anxious to do that, but even more to get away from the subject of whom she reminded him.

He glanced at his watch. "I just have to take Michelangelo out for a walk first."

"Why don't you bring him with us."

He looked at her curiously. "You wouldn't mind."

"Of course not. I love dogs." She really did. Even as Samantha Day, she loved animals.

"And he loves nothing more than long walks around the city and is, in fact, a canine expert at waiting for me whenever I go into places he can't. Thanks. I'll get him and be back in a moment," he said and started to walk toward the door.

She frowned. "Do you live so close?"

He stopped and pointed down to the floor. "Right below this apartment."

"Really?"

He nodded. "I redid the apartment right after Lorenzo finished with this one. That was three years ago. And how we became acquainted personally."

For the first time, she looked around at her surroundings, noticing the artistry that could have only come from a very good interior designer. "Who would have expected such a modern apartment in such an old building? It's beautiful." It was. She had only had eyes for the view when she first walked in, but now she let her gaze wander around the airy penthouse. It was bathed in light with open spaces that easily filled up with the golden Tuscan sunlight. A pair of Italian sling chairs set the tone in the living area. Contemporary and simple. Nothing dark. Silk covered the sofa. Only blinds were on the windows, no curtains to hinder the view or shut out the light. And there was no clutter.

He nodded. "I liked it so much I had mine designed by the same person."

"So your apartment looks just like this one?"

"Except that it's not on three levels and there's a bit more clutter. And plants." He smiled sheepishly. "And dog hair that my housekeeper is always chasing."

"Just sounds lived-in to me." As beautiful as this apartment was, it didn't have that feeling. It looked like it was ready for a magazine crew to come in and take pictures of it. She reached for her purse. "I'll come with you. I can't wait to meet your dog and get out into that city."

Domenico laughed, a sound that came from low in his throat. "I have a feeling that they both can't wait to meet you, either."

Chapter 5

Firenze was everything and more than what Florence had expected. It was large squares filled with people, medieval churches filled with people, arched bridges filled with people, large and small museums filled with people, long streets filled with people, quaint alleyways filled with people, beautiful restaurants filled with people, and stores of all kinds — both designer and Ma and Pa — filled with people: people from around the world and not one of whom recognized Florence as being Samantha Day.

And Florence loved it, loved the anonymity, and loved hearing all the different languages being spoken as she walked over the Ponto Vecchio — aptly named Old Bridge since the bridge as it was in its present form had stood from 1345. And she loved ambling down the Piazza d'Uffizi with its outdoor gallery of nineteenth century statues of Firenze's famous citizens in niches built into the Galleria degli Uffizi – Uffizi Art Gallery — on her way to the Piazza della Signoria — the traditional center and political hub of the city. The fourteenth century *loggia* — porch — located across from the Palazzo Vecchio was an outdoor art gallery with original artwork from as far back as the fourth century B.C.

But spying Brunelleschi's enormous fifteenth century dome that topped the *duomo* — cathedral — as she and Domenico walked the many roads and alleys of the city stirred her heart and made her catch her breath each time she caught a glimpse of it. At least half a football field in length and more than an entire field in height, it seemed to almost be floating above the city, like a vision from heaven. And if the *duomo* wasn't visible, then the elegant lines of its bell tower, designed by Giotto in the early 1300s with its iridescent marble covering, was. The structures were magnificent, and each time she saw them from yet another angle between the golden tones of the city's buildings, whom they were built to glorify — Jesus Christ — somehow seemed to sink deeper and deeper into her soul. The reaction she was having to being in this city of churches and Christian artwork was continuing the chain of events that had started when she first received Domenico's letter. Combined

86

with her daily Bible reading time — the last thing she did each night before falling to sleep — the change it was bringing to her was all a bit mind-boggling.

But something else that boggled her mind was walking through the quaint medieval city with Domenico Ferretti by her side.

That first afternoon started a trend that they continued for each succeeding day of the week. And the more time they spent together walking the streets of their ancestors and sharing noon meals together at outdoor cafés in the city's piazzas and at candlelit restaurants filled with Tuscan ambiance at night, the more they grew to both like and respect one another. In a very short time, Domenico Ferretti became Florence's very best friend.

Florence's first thought that he was very similar to her grandpop proved to be correct. He was a man who lived his life according to the precepts of the Bible. And as they were standing before the eastern doors of the octagonal Baptistry — the oldest building in the city — looking at Old Testament scenes that Ghiberti had masterly sculpted in bas-reliefs from gilded bronze, Florence realized that that had become something very important to her.

She suspected that Domenico was a man in the way God meant for boys to grow into men: like her grandpop and beloved *babbo,* one who always had God in the center of his heart. It had been a long time since Florence had been around such a complete man. Ten years.

"It took Ghiberti twenty-eight years to complete these doors," Domenico said from her side, startling her from her reverie.

"Twenty-eight! That's longer than I've been alive by one year."

Domenico nodded. "Michelangelo — the man I mean," he qualified and looked down at his dog, who sat by their feet, and smiled, "stood right here before the original ones — which are now in the Museo dell'Opera del Duomo — the Cathedral Museum — for protection — and said, 'They are so fine that they might fittingly stand as the Porta del Paradiso.' "

" 'The Gates of Paradise,' " she murmured.

He squeezed her hand. They had been holding hands for the past four days, something that felt perfect and right, like an extension of her own self. "Very good, *carissima.* Your ability to pick up Italian so quickly amazes me."

She beamed and tilted her head toward his. "I've had a good teacher." He had been helping her add to her smattering of Italian all week. But other than that, she knew that she was only incorporating the same technique to learn the language as she did when studying scripts. She looked toward the door again and its ten panels, most of which were subdivided into several subjects. "I can see why Michelangelo would say that. These are so moving." She pointed to the first panel in the upper left corner of the huge door that depicted the creation of Adam and Eve. "Even if I didn't know the story, I could understand what is going on here. It's almost like a children's picture book."

He chuckled. "I like that. Ghiberti's golden doors compared to a picture book."

She was afraid she had offended him. In a city of artwork, she knew that these doors were one of its most prized. "I mean no disrespect."

"None taken. Honestly. I like the analogy." He indicated the doors. "It was Renaissance man's answer to the value of teaching through pictures. All people, both young and old, saw them. In a day when books were scarce, they learned Bible stories this way."

"Exactly." She was glad that he under-stood what she meant. She indicated the lower left corner of the panel and recited the verses she had read just the previous night in Genesis. " 'The Lord God formed the man from the dust of the ground and breathed into his nostrils the breath of life, and the man became a living being.' " She paused for a moment and gazed at the work that showed Adam being literally raised from the dust of the earth by God. "That is so obviously what is happening here. Makes me wonder why people have a problem with evolution and the Bible's story of creation. It's so obvious here. Man was finely sculpted just as God wanted him to be and could now receive the breath of life."

He looked at her and, with awe in his voice, said, "I've never thought of it like that." He shook his head. "You told me the day you arrived in Firenze that you had lost both God and your faith somewhere along the way. But after all these days we've spent together, you haven't seemed that way to me at all."

She grimaced. "I've changed . . . a lot, Domenico, since coming to Firenze." She shrugged her shoulders and wondered if now was the time to tell him everything about her, including the Samantha Day part. She decided not. As with other times, it just didn't seem to fit in with the moment. "Something about this city" — she waved her arm out in an all-encompassing way — "its churches, its beautiful works of art, all seem to guide my thoughts in a God-centered way, one it hasn't traveled in many years. That so many people — smart, talented people — like Signor Ghiberti who believed so greatly in God above and in His redemptive work through Jesus Christ that he spent twenty-eight years making these panels that visually tell the Bible stories" — she pointed back to Ghiberti's masterpiece — "makes me think. Think about God."

"I know what you mean, although a lot of the work you see around the city wasn't necessarily done because of faith. As much as I — as a Florentine — might not want to admit it, a great deal was commissioned just so that the rich of the city could show off to the world their wealth." He shrugged. "It was good for business. Not in every case, of course, and I'm not referring to Ghiberti, whose knowledge about the Bible stories had to have been extensive to have created this, but often."

"How cynical."

"Artists created what was asked of them because they had to eat." He smiled and, looking at his watch, started guiding her and Michelangelo away from the doors. "Come on." He looked up at the overcast sky. "I'll take you to see the work of a man for whom there is absolutely no doubt about his love of God."

"It's more wonderful in person than any card or poster could ever depict." She spoke a few minutes later, as they stood in the southern corridor on the upper floor of the convent of San Marco — now a museum devoted to the fifteenth century painter Fra Angelico — looking with awe at the fresco entitled *The Annunciation*.

"I knew you would like seeing it in person."

"Like it? I stand in awe of it. I can almost feel Mary's joy, surprise, fright, and amazement that an angel should visit her and with such amazing news. It's so serene and filled with diaphanous light. And Gabriel's wings seem to be made up of rainbows from the sky."

"The rainbow of God's promise, perhaps?"

She pulled her gaze away from the painting, not an easy thing to do, and turned to him. "The promise He made to Noah after He flooded the world? Telling that He would never flood the earth again?"

"Maybe."

She nodded and he could tell from the way she rearranged her glasses and pursed her lips that she was really thinking about it. That was something she often did. And it was something he loved about her. Giovanna had claimed to be a Christian, and yet she had always shied away from talking about deeper theological topics. He liked how a love of discussing things of God was something he and Florence seemed to share.

But that wasn't all he loved about Florence.

He loved how open and truthful she was about everything, but mostly about her search to rediscover the faith of her childhood. She didn't know it, but she and her *nonno* were so similar. He was only certain that Florence had never been as mean to people as Lorenzo had been.

"Yes, maybe," she continued after a moment and turned back to the painting. Holding her hand out as if to touch the colors of the wings, but of course not doing so, she said, "I don't claim to be an expert, but I've never seen an angel's wings painted like the rainbow before."

"And yet, according to the Bible, angels are fantastically beautiful creatures. Why not colors?"

"Why indeed? Fra Angelico must have been a very special Christian to think about that."

"The art historian, painter, and architect Giorgio Vasari, who was born just a little more than half a century after Fra Angelico, wrote that he was 'a simple and most holy man.' "

She motioned to the paintings that surrounded them. "Even though Fra Angelico has been gone for more than five hundred years, his work lets us know him. His soul was definitely at peace. No disturbing or agitating elements could have been in the man he was." She waved her hand in front of her in a dismissing way. "I don't mean that living the life of a medieval monk he didn't have problems — everyone on earth has problems of one sort or another — but he seemed to let God take charge of those problems. He would have had to, in order to execute works that seem so God-inspired, so much a part of heaven, works that seem to be not just for the glorification of God but also for the edification of his fellow humans, something to help us in our . . ." She paused and frowned, the frown whereby fine lines crinkled her forehead and made her seem so familiar to him. Sometimes when she smiled he had that impression, too. And he didn't mean just because of her *nonno*. "I don't know," she continued, bringing his thoughts back to their conversation. "Something to help us see God?"

"Exactly. That's the reason he painted the monks' bedrooms, their cells, and the walls of these corridors: To help his brothers in their devotions."

She walked over to cell number one. "Imagine having *Noli me Tangere*" — she indicated the painting depicting Jesus appearing to Mary Magdalene outside of the tomb on Easter morning — "to help you in your devotions?"

"Would you like a copy of it" — he indicated the direction of the corridor — "or of *The Annunciation*?"

She gasped, a sound that once again seemed so known to him. But the way she looked at him, as if the idea that she could own a copy of such a work of art had never occurred to her, was only as familiar as their days together had been. "I would. I really would."

"Which one would you like?"

"You choose." She took his hand and squeezed it, and Domenico felt his blood pound through his veins. It felt so right, so good, to make Florence happy. She was so grateful for the littlest of things. "But you don't have to go to all that trouble, Domenico. I'll look for a print."

"No, I want to." What he had in mind was far more than just a print bought from the museum's store. But he wanted that to be a surprise. "Besides, that's what dear Fra Angelico would have wanted. Even after five hundred years, his artwork is still helping his brothers and sisters in the Lord."

Emotion gathered in her eyes in the form of tears. She could only nod in agreement. At this moment Florence didn't know how she had lived the last ten years without the faith that was becoming so much a part of her since first receiving Domenico's letter or . . . how she had lived without Domenico.

Both having faith and Domenico by her side brought out the very best in her. And she was beginning to realize that the very best in her was . . . Florence Celini.

"Thank you. I'd like that," she said,

when she could find her voice. She would replace the Pablo Picasso she had in the bedroom of her Manhattan apartment with the print Domenico would give to her. That print would be far more valuable to her than that original work of art by the twentieth century artist. First because it would be a gift from Domenico and second because she would, as Fra Angelico had intended for all who looked upon his work, be edified by it in her devotions. It would always help her remember what was important in life.

Compassion, kindness, humility, gentleness, patience, forgiveness, love . . .

Love . . .

She slanted her eyes up to Domenico as they walked arm in arm under the arched porticos of the convent turned museum toward the exit.

Love . . .

She *loved* this man.

She didn't know how it was possible to love a man she hadn't known even existed two weeks earlier, but in her heart — the heart that had, only the previous night, welcomed God to be a part of it again after an eviction of ten years — she knew that she did.

But she knew, too, that before she told

Domenico anything — even about her life-changing decision of the previous night — she had to tell him about Samantha Day. And finally answer the question of recognition that she had so often seen in his eyes. Even a few minutes earlier when Samantha Day's world famous gasp had escaped her lips.

She owed him the total truth before she could declare her love. Because love was based on truth, and without total honesty between them, there could never be a future. And a future with Domenico in it was what she wanted.

She slanted her eyes over at him.

Such a future seemed like pure Tuscan gold to her.

Chapter 6

The next day Florence awoke to a sky that
was ominous. But unlike when the persona
of Samantha Day had ruled her life, and not
God, it didn't bother her in the least. Her
soul was sunny. She was in love with a wonderful man, and they were going out on the
best "date" Florence could now imagine:
they were going to Sunday morning church
service together.

Since it looked like the Tuscan sky was
going to pour some of its ample supply of
rain upon the land, Domenico decided to
drive them.

"How can you decide which church to
go to in this city of churches?" Florence
asked as they drove over the Amerigo
Vespucci Bridge just as the first drops of
rain started to fall from the windy autumn
sky. The surface of the Arno River was
dancing with the big fat drops of liquid.
Florence decided then that she liked
Firenze in the rain just as much as she did
in the sunshine. It was cozy.

"Today it was an easy choice. St. James

is the American church at Firenze." He flashed her his smile. "I want you to be able to understand everything, so it's the only choice, really."

"The service is in English?" She hadn't expected that. It thrilled her that after her decision of two nights earlier, she was going to hear a sermon she could understand. She was almost craving it.

Amusement glinted in his eyes. "Totally."

But what else she hadn't anticipated was how the pastor's sermon seemed to speak directly to her heart. It was all about forgiveness. What stunned Florence the most, however, was that she didn't sit in the congregation as he spoke about forgiveness and consider whether she would forgive her paternal grandfather for the estrangement as much as whether her *maternal* grandfather — her beloved grandpop — could forgive *her* for spurning all his love, prayers, and advice throughout the last ten years. The dear man had given her nothing but love, and she had returned it by giving him only obligatory phone calls a few times a year while pursuing a lifestyle that was, if not exactly harmful, not good for her, either.

"Grandpop," she mouthed out and

fished around in her purse for a tissue, as conviction over her behavior washed through her like the rain outside did the city streets. She wished she could hug the dear old man right this minute and beg his pardon. She glanced at her watch. She would call him as soon as it was morning in Texas.

Domenico leaned close to her and, with his eyes full of compassionate concern, offered her a linen handkerchief from his pocket. It only made her tears fall faster. She remembered how her grandpop always had a supply of fresh linen handkerchiefs to offer crying souls touched by worship service on Sunday mornings, too.

With a tremulous smile, she took it. She held it to her nose and inhaled its special aroma, a blend of Domenico's aftershave and that fresh laundry smell, before she lifted it to her eyes and dabbed at their corners. The service ended shortly afterward, and it was with a grateful heart that she let Domenico lead her back to the car and with even more relief that he drove through the rain-soaked streets without saying a word.

Guilt over having mistreated her grandpop still swept through her. Her grandpop had never given her anything but love. He had taken her in when she was orphaned and had never made her feel as if she were intruding in his life. Not once. And since her grandma had died about the time her parents had married, that meant all the care for a seven year old had fallen upon him. And how had she repaid him? By not only turning her back on the unconditional love he had given to her but on the faith of their common ancestors, one that had produced such wonderful people as he and his daughter — Florence's mother.

"Do you want to tell me about it?" Domenico asked with that kind, gentle voice that musically caressed her soul. It was only then she realized that he had stopped the car and that they were parked near the old bridge, the Ponte Vecchio.

She nodded. She did want to tell him. Everything. It was time to tell all. About her grandpop and how she had behaved toward him, but even more . . . about her career and stage persona, Samantha Day. She nodded and pointed out at the gray September day. "It's not raining now. Can we walk onto the bridge?" The Ponte Vecchio, with its jewelry shops from the Middle Ages, had become one of her favorite "thinking spots" in Firenze. She loved standing in the middle of it and gazing out at the Fiume Arno below as the river wended its way under the many arched bridges on its inexorable way to the sea.

He smiled. "Just what I had in mind. We'll probably find it deserted, too, since the combination of rain and it being Sunday morning will keep most people inside."

He came around and opened her door for her. Stepping out of the car, she gave a slight shiver as the rain-cooled air touched her hot skin. She fastened her wine-colored cable knit cardigan sweater closer around her body. "It's chilly."

Putting his arm around her shoulder, he gently pulled her close to him. His warmth enveloped her like a down comforter might, and yet, in a comforting human way that was a million times better. "How's that?"

She leaned against him as naturally as breathing. "Perfect." Of its own volition her arm went around his waist, and she smiled up at him. They walked past the Mannelli Tower, which had been built in medieval days to defend the bridge, before walking beside the shops that both lined, and, with the use of support timber brackets, overhung most of the bridge.

"I'm glad the butchers were evicted from the bridge back in Duke Ferdinando's days," he said. "One of the wiser things for a ruler to have done." There was a dry humor in Domenico's voice as he motioned to the mostly still-shuttered windows of the goldsmith and jewelry stores that were old-world, unaffected ambiance at its best.

"These shops *are* much more pleasant," she agreed.

They walked over to the center of the bridge just below the middle arch that supported the Vasari Corridor — that private walkway that had allowed members of the Medici family to move about between their various residences without having to walk onto the streets below and mix with the crowds.

Since it still wasn't raining, only slightly misting, they moved to the uncovered opposite side and, with their arms around one another, they gazed out past the ducks that were paddling around on the surface of the river to the Ponte Santa Trinita, the closest bridge to the west of Ponte Vecchio. The three other western bridges could be seen off beyond it, all lined up like dominoes.

"Did you know that Ponte Vecchio was

the only bridge not destroyed by the re-treating Germans during World War II?"

She gasped and pointed to Ponte Santa Trinita. "You mean that bridge is new?" With its elegant lines and elegant statues situated at each end, it seemed to have been built during Renaissance days.

"In a way. After the original bridge — dating from 1562 — was blown up in 1944, the Florentines decided to rebuild it exactly as it had been. Engineers used copies of sixteenth century tools and stone from the Boboli quarry, and the bridge was again reopened in 1958. Michelangelo was credited with having designed the original, the one this emulates."

She slanted her eyes up to him and quipped, "Your dog? What an amazing beast."

"Right," he chuckled.

She looked back at the bridge. "Michel-angelo Buonarroti . . . no wonder it's so beautiful."

He nodded. "The statues of the four sea-sons are the original ones. They were dredged up from the river."

The pastor's sermon about forgiveness came back to her. "Living really is all about forgiveness, isn't it?"

"Are you talking about the people of this

city forgiving the Germans for destroying their bridges — works of art all of them," he qualified in the manner of a true Florentine who had been very hurt by the bridges' destruction, "or are you referring to your having to forgive your *nonno?*"

Her mouth crooked in a wry line. "Actually neither. I'm thinking about whether my grandpop — the man who raised me from the age of seven — will ever be able to forgive *me,*" she touched her hand to her chest, "for spurning both his careful Christian counsel and the unconditional love he has always offered to me."

His gaze narrowed with wary censure. "I didn't know you had problems with your grandpop."

She stiffened at the challenging statement. "I don't. I mean," she shrugged and tried to explain. "I hurt him when I didn't pursue the life of faith he had raised me to follow. I know that he never approved of my moving to New York and of, well, my lifestyle. And because of that, I have been kind of avoiding him. It's just that . . . I always feel so guilty whenever I'm around him. I know he disapproves."

She was glad when he seemed to understand. Tipping his head to one side he said, "A very wise man once taught a prayer. Part of it went like this, " 'Forgive us our debts, as we also have forgiven our debtors . . .' "

She remembered that one. She had prayed it every night when a little girl. With her grandpop sitting by her side. "The Lord's prayer," she murmured.

He nodded. "God wants to forgive us all. But He will not forgive the guilt of those who knowingly refuse to admit their sin. Like the pastor pointed out in today's teaching, the key to forgiveness is that a person asks to be forgiven. Your *nonno* has asked that you forgive him; the Germans asked that the people of the city of Firenze forgive them; you want to ask your grandpop to forgive you; but the greatest example, of course, is the original one: people can ask God to forgive them their sins in Jesus' name, and because of what Jesus did when He hung on that cross, God does. Forgive us, I mean. Forgiveness begins with people asking for it, asking of God and asking of one another. That's when the healing process can begin."

His words reminded her of the verses her parents had written to her in their letter. She knew them by heart now, so she recited them. " 'Bear with each other and forgive whatever grievances you may have against one another. Forgive as the Lord forgave you.' "

He looked at her curiously. "You know, after our first phone conversation I thought about you and your situation with your *nonno* in terms of those verses."

Her parents' verses? Her heart seemed to skip a beat. "What do you mean?"

He guided her out into the center of the bridge where the dome of the *duomo* — a beacon to Christianity — rose above the narrow city streets and golden buildings into the Tuscan sky. It was as striking and awe inspiring on this rainy day as it was on the sunniest. "I was looking out my office window at that and considered that the only way that you would ever be able to forgive your *nonno* was if you were to "clothe" yourself with the virtues of compassion, kindness, humility, and patience talked about by St. Paul in the verse preceding the one you just spoke."

She squeezed her eyes shut at the feeling of destiny that swept through her. "My grandpop would say, Domenico, that this is a . . . 'God thing.' " Funny how she remembered that expression after all these years. But her grandpop had a way of making everything simple.

"What do you mean?"

She explained. "After talking to you, I had some decisions to make. Not only about whether I would come here but," she bit her lower lip, "about other things, too." She would tell him about Samantha Day, just not right now. She didn't want Samantha Day to intrude upon this moment. Now it was more important to tell him about finding her parents' letter in the Bible and the verses. She did. "So you see now why it's a God thing?"

After a thoughtful moment, he nodded. "God was using the same exact verses to speak to our hearts even though we were so far away from each other and really didn't even know one another." He looked at her as if a piece of a puzzle had just fallen into place. "And that's why you seemed to have changed from the first conversation to the next."

She nodded, but could only hope that when she told him about what else had happened during that time — that she had decided to come to Firenze as Florence Celini and to leave Samantha Day behind — that he would "wear" the virtues, too . . . and forgive her not telling him sooner. *Is now the time to tell him, Lord, now that we are talking about forgiveness?*

But when he suddenly turned and

walked over to the edge of the bridge to look out toward Ponte Santa Trinita again, she knew that it wasn't. He obviously had something on his mind that he wanted to tell her.

She went to stand next to him.

"Last year, Florence, I almost married."

Her eyes widened. That was the last thing she had expected him to say. If he had told her that he was going to swim across the Atlantic, she wouldn't have been any more surprised. A slight tremor went through her. She couldn't help it. But to have met a *married* Domenico Ferretti at the airport the previous week would have been a tragedy to her.

An ironic smile twisted his full lips. "I fancied myself very much in love." His face turned as stormy looking as the sky that looked as if it were ready to soon let loose with more rain.

She slightly shook her head. Why was he telling her this? And why now?

Interpreting her question he put his hand up in a lawyer way that said he had a point to make. To bear with him. She did. "The woman I loved was not who she seemed to be. She had only been acting as if she loved me. When in fact what she loved was the lifestyle she hoped to marry upon 'catching' me." He turned to fully face her, and the pain from that time was still visible in the deepness of his eyes, in the tautness of his stance. "She had deceived me. Acting a role in order to catch herself a husband of old Florentine lineage."

Florence's blood seemed to stop running. *Acting a role?* Thank God — and she meant it literally — she hadn't said anything to him about Samantha Day. What would he think of her when he found out about her stage persona?

But it was different.

Totally.

She wasn't trying to "catch" him. The fact that she had fallen in love with him had had nothing to do with her having spurned the persona of Samantha Day while in Firenze. But why was he telling her this now? What was his point?

She forced herself to listen as he continued. "But do you know what the worst part about her entire deception was?" She knew it was a rhetorical question so she waited for him to continue even though all she wanted to do was shout out, "What, what?"

"She never, not once, asked for my forgiveness. She acted as if she hadn't done anything wrong. In fact," his voice lowered, and she could hear the pain in it, "she turned everything around to make it sound as if *I* was the one who had hurt *her*."

Now she understood his point. It was all about the process of forgiveness. She was glad that he had shared it with her. Placing her arms around his neck she hugged him tightly to her, wishing she could hug all the pain away. Into his ear she said, "I'm so sorry, Domenico."

She felt her heart flutter like leaves falling from a tree, and he hugged her back tightly and yet with control. It was as if he had found his home in her arms, the one woman in the world who he knew would always be there for him. It made her feel special in a way she had never experienced before. She hoped that he always felt that way. She wanted to be that woman, *his* woman. For always.

As she pressed her nose into the softly scented skin of his masculine neck, she knew that she felt the same way. It was his arms she would always seek for comfort, for support, for love. Combined with everything else about him, his sense of dignity, his faith, his arms just felt so right to her. They fit together.

When he released her and took half a

step back, a poignant smile lifted the corners of his mouth, and reaching up, he ran his fingers in a caressing way down her cheek. His fingertips felt like cotton against her cool skin. "She never even said that much."

Florence squeezed her eyes together. For the pain he had experienced the previous year, for the pain she was afraid he would feel upon learning about her, well, kind of deception. *Dear Lord,* she prayed within herself, *please Lord, help him to forgive me. Help him to understand that I love him not for anything temporal that he can give me but for who he is . . . and that . . . I had to leave Samantha Day behind in order to find Florence Celini. Please, Lord.*

Exhilaration flowed through her when she understood what she was doing. Praying . . . She realized that her mouth had dropped open when he looked at her curiously.

"What is it?"

"I . . ." She let out a sound that was a cross between laughter and amazement and shook her head vaguely. "I was just praying . . . and . . . I did a few moments earlier, too. I haven't done that in . . . years."

"Praying?" He smiled, his eyes crinkling

at their corners in a pleased way. "About what?"

"Us," she whispered.

"Umm . . ." His husky voice was like a caress. "I like the way that sounds." And slowly, as slowly as little drops of rain now fell from the sky, he lowered his lips to hers, and the magic, the wonder, of knowing that those lips belonged to the man she loved filled Florence. In her work she had kissed many men — some of the most sought-after men in the world today — but those kisses had been like kissing cardboard compared to the joy, the delight, the overwhelming feeling of having found her home, as Domenico's lips moved against hers in a dance of oneness that was as ancient as that probably experienced by Adam and Eve. And Florence knew as they stood on the bridge that her ancestors had walked over for generations upon generations that she had indeed found her home, her place in this world. It was by Domenico's side.

Domenico lifted his lips just far enough from hers to say those three most giving words, "I love you."

"I love you back," she whispered, knowing that she had never spoken any more truthfully.

Bells started ringing all around the ancient city of Firenze, with the *duomo*'s huge bell leading them all. Looking around, Florence and Domenico laughed together.

"Do you think that's a sign?"

"Not even Hollywood could have orchestrated that timing better."

"No," he agreed. "This is God's timing." He paused, then said, "And I have something else to tell you."

"What could be better than 'I love you'?" she asked, still feeling the warm touch of his lips upon her own.

He kissed the tip of her nose. "I didn't say it was better. But it *is* good. Your *nonno* is going to be back tomorrow."

She nodded. "It really is God's timing, Domenico." She paused and explained. "Even yesterday, I wouldn't have been ready to meet him. But today, after listening to that sermon and talking to you and knowing that it is up to me to ask my grandpop to forgive me, I know exactly what I will do with my . . . *nonno*."

With a slight catch to his voice that matched the twist of his head he said, "That's the first time you've called him *Nonno*."

She knew it was true. "I couldn't before.

115

He didn't seem like a *nonno* to me. But now, having lived in his apartment and walked his city, I feel privileged to know that there is a man to whom I'm related who wants to meet me. He made a mistake." She shrugged her shoulders. "I've made mistakes, too. With my grandpop, and well," she sighed out deeply, "with many other things."

"So will you forgive him?" She could tell from the hopeful sound in his voice how much he really loved the old man.

"No." At the sight of the disappointment that sliced across his classical features, she quickly explained. "Since, through your letter, he's already *asked* that I forgive him, I already have. It's not something I have to do in the future — tomorrow — when I meet him. It's done. My forgiveness is his. Now I just want to get to know him."

With that voice, that deep husky voice that did nothing but get better sounding to her ears, Domenico repeated, "I love you, Florence."

"I love you, too, Domenico." She did. More than anything or anyone in the world she loved this man. And she thanked God for the letter from her parents that had taught her to "wear" the virtues of compassion, kindness, gentleness and patience, forgiveness and love, which had in turn taught her how to be a woman of faith again — one who Domenico Ferretti could love.

Chapter 7

Florence called her grandpop the minute the clock showed that it was seven in the morning in Texas. When she heard his dear voice on the phone with its sweet Texan drawl, she nearly started crying. But pulling once again on her training, she managed to keep her decorum and to tell him all that had happened to her since receiving his manila envelope with the letter from Italy enclosed. When she told him that she had, somewhere among finding her parents' letter, reading her Bible, walking the streets of Florence with all its artwork glorifying Jesus on the arm of a man who reminded her of him in belief, finally become the woman of faith he had raised her to be, he called her by her name, Florence. It was the first time he had since she had taken on the name of Samantha Day.

"I always knew my Florence would return someday," he said, his voice deep and gravelly with age and sentiment, but filled, too, with all the love for which a granddaughter could ever ask.

"Grandpop . . . can you ever forgive me for . . . everything . . . ?"

"How can I not forgive you when my Lord has forgiven me for so much more? Of course I forgive you. Especially since you ask me to do so. Thank you for that."

There it was again . . . the asking of another's forgiveness . . . just as the pastor and Domenico had said yesterday. "Oh, Grandpop . . . I've missed you." She had, more than she ever even realized.

"You know, Little Darling," he called her by his pet name for her, making the tears that had been swimming in her eyes brim over and ride down her cheeks. "I never minded your pursuing a career in acting. What I didn't like was how you let acting change you. There are many fine actors working in Hollywood and in New York who don't let the job change them — change their belief and their faith in God. You did, though. That's what I didn't like. Acting is a career. It's not your life. You are Florence Celini. Not Samantha Day."

"I know that now, Grandpop."

"I love you, Little Darling."

"I love you, too, Grandpop."

"Come and visit me soon?"

She knew what it took for him to ask that of her. She loved him even more for the giving of that gift. This was a man — a man after God's own heart — one who would never hold a grudge. "I will. And . . . I might even bring someone special with me."

"He's like me in his faith, you say?" She could hear the smile in her grandpop's voice, could just imagine the soft crinkles around his eyes, the way his lips turned down, not up, in his own special way of smiling. "Who says God doesn't answer prayers?"

"Not me, Grandpop. Not me." And as she hung up the phone she knew that she would never question that again.

Domenico drove her through the fragrant hills above Florence to the *palazzo* — palace — in which her father had grown up and where her Italian grandfather now waited for her. Located on forty acres in the Tuscan Apennines, the villa, built in the sixteenth century, was surrounded by groves of olive trees and vineyards on terraced fields, with reaching cypress trees lining the long drive leading up to the grand entrance. With its arched porticoes and numerous Renaissance fountains, this *palazzo* made her Central Park apartment in Manhattan seem like a trailer home.

She eyed what could only be a draw-bridge that connected the main entrance hall to a stone bridge that led to the front garden and frowned as bits of misty memory mixed with the feelings she was getting from this actual place to move together within her mind. "I've . . . seen . . . this house before," she whispered to Domenico.

She felt him glance over at her. "What do you mean?"

Sitting up closer to the windshield she said, "Not with my eyes, but with my mind. My father . . . he always told me stories about a young princess who lived in a house that was filled with all the good and wonderful things any little girl could want. It was huge but friendly, had a red-tiled roof with a tower," she said, pointing to the highest point of the house — a tower that sat in the middle above three arched porticoes, "a draw bridge, and a garden that had the most wonderful maze made of tall, thick bushes."

"There is a maze here," he motioned to the back and side of the house. "Over there. It's very old. Centuries."

She felt ready to jump out of her skin. *Of course there was!* "And there is a room on the second floor with a portrait of a famous ancestor on horseback and" — she held up her hand as if moving it over what she saw in her mind's eye — "an elaborate grisaille fresco frieze with scrolls crowning the brocade-covered walls and a Renaissance-style ceiling. It's called the grand reception room but my *babbo* always said it was really the throne room where the little princess used to hide behind the velvet curtains and listen to all the events affecting her world take place."

"That describes the room on the second floor perfectly." There was the same amazement in his voice now that had been in hers a moment before. "Your father told you about his home? Through storytelling?"

She swallowed the lump that had formed in her throat. "I . . . didn't know he was describing *his* childhood home. I thought it was a magic fairy land filled with everything good and pure and right."

"I think perhaps that's what he hoped it might one day become for you."

She nodded. "But he knew that until his father changed, that it could never be so." She reached over for his hand. "Please, Domenico, pray with me about this reunion."

Pulling the car to a stop in the shade of a

four-story-high cypress tree, Domenico turned to her and to the sound of birds and insects singing all around them and to the wind softly blowing its melodious tune over the sun-drenched ancient land he wrapped her hands in his own and they prayed. They were one in spirit as God intended man and woman to be when they came to Him . . . together. "Dear Father, please bless this reunion between Florence and her *nonno*, Lorenzo. Let it be the very reunion that Cosimo had been praying for even when his daughter, Florence, was just a little girl. A reconciliation that is full of your light and grace and love, one that brings all the good Cosimo dreamed might someday come to this land where his little princess — his daughter — might be happy among its walls. In Jesus' precious name we pray. Amen."

Florence squeezed his hands. "That is really just what my *babbo* was hoping," she whispered. "That someday I would come here and find it the happy place he described in his storytelling."

"And that could only have happened if your *nonno* changed."

"God's grace," she murmured. Then, looking up at the imposing lines of the *palazzo* she said, "And God's timing. It took many years but Nonno has changed. And I have, too. And now I'm here in this house that my father must have loved very much." She flashed him her brightest smile, not even caring when that look of question crossed over his face. Samantha Day wasn't even important any longer. Loving Domenico and meeting the ancestor who waited for her in that storybook palace was all that presently mattered. "I'm ready."

The big, but compact, man who welcomed her with opened arms and with tears of remorse in his eyes, begging over and over for her forgiveness, was not at all the person she had expected her *nonno* to be. She had expected a frail, autocratic man with pinched lips who had to, in spite of God's work in his heart, swallow his pride in order to ask for her forgiveness. Instead, she was introduced to a man she was thrilled to call her second grandfather. She liked him immediately.

"What you see in me, *mia cara,* is a work only God could have performed. I was a bitter, hateful, unforgiving man consumed with materialistic pursuits. Until all the prayers offered up for my salvation and all the churches and artwork in Firenze glorifying God converged with that still small voice in my soul to speak to my heart." His handsome head, with its full covering of white hair, hung down, and he spoke with so much emotion that between it and his strong Italian accent, Florence almost couldn't understand him. But the fact that everything he described had also touched her heart helped her to understand. "I only wish I had comprehended what Cosimo was trying to tell me all those years ago. So much pain could have been avoided. So much harm . . . all caused by me."

Florence's gaze sought that of Domenico's. She could tell how much he hated seeing his friend like this. She understood. Even though this was the man who had been so mean to her mother and father, she felt the same way.

She tentatively reached out to softly place her hand on her grandfather's arm. "Nonno —"

She jumped at how suddenly he looked up at her. Was even more startled when among the sorrowful lines a smile split across his face. It was like the sun cutting through clouds on a dark wintry day. "That is the first time anyone has ever called me that. Nonno . . . Thank you for forgiving me enough to do so. I know I don't deserve the honor the title bestows."

Tears pricked at her eyes and made her throat close up. "But you are my *nonno*. And because of that . . . because . . . you gave life to my *babbo* . . . I love you."

He shook his head. "I don't deserve your love."

"How many of us ever deserve the love another wants to give us, Nonno?"

"But I am the most undeserving of all."

"I think St. Peter might have felt that way after he disowned the Lord three times the night Jesus was betrayed. And look what Peter went on to do."

He looked at her deeply, but she knew he wasn't seeing her face, but rather searching for bits and pieces of the young man he had disowned so long ago, his son. "You sounded just like Cosimo when you said that. He always knew about things of God, too."

She had to set him straight about how she had been living her life and the part he had played in her changing it. "Nonno, until I received Domenico's letter," — she motioned toward Domenico — "telling me about your wanting me in your life . . . and that you had changed . . . I was a very different person, too. More like you had been than my father had been, actually."

Incredulity entered his eyes, eyes that she had immediately noticed were indeed a mirror of her own, the exact same green with aquamarine outer circles. Looking at them she could finally understand why people sometimes considered her own scary. Her *nonno*'s eyes were intense in a soul-piercing way. She had to assume that hers were the same. "I don't believe it," he finally said.

She nodded. "Domenico's letter reminded me about the Bible my parents had given to me when I was a little girl. I found it and a letter they had written to me which had verses from Colossians —"

She stopped speaking when he held up his hand. He had a commanding way of doing it that she considered had probably always made people pause. "Wait a minute. They gave me a Bible, too. One I had forgotten about until two months ago when my housekeeper found it and brought it to me. It, too, had verses from Colossians written in it."

Another God thing! She looked up at Domenico, and understanding what she was thinking, he put his hand on her shoulder and, with a soft smile, nodded his head. Turning back to her *nonno*, she slowly recited the verses she had found in her Bible. Before she was done speaking them, she knew from the tears that were streaming down the lines time — and his having spent most of it in anger — had wrought in her *nonno*'s face that they were the exact same words.

"My Cosimo and," he paused and heaved a deep sigh full of remorse, "the good woman he loved — Mary, your dear mother — have reached down from heaven to lead us both down the correct path, the one whereby we walk with God."

"Yes, Nonno." A faint tremor quivered through Florence. "They most definitely have."

To say that the next hour was wonderful would be to take something away from the time the three of them spent together. It was a time of deepening love and understanding and one of bonding that they all knew could only be achieved through the grace of God.

Florence didn't think anything in the world could ever encroach on her happiness that day.

But when her *nonno*'s housekeeper walked in with a tray laden with refreshments and, upon taking one look at her, blurted out, "You're Samantha Day!" she learned how tenuous happiness was, even with God's grace hovering around. People's emotions, and in this case that of Domenico's, could always be counted upon to impose upon it.

With three sets of eyes trained upon her, Florence could only nod her head.

"I knew it. I knew it," the housekeeper blubbered out, as enthusiastic as the best of fans and almost dropping the silver tray in the process. "I go to all your movies. All of them. Did you think changing the color of your hair or wearing glasses could hide who you really are? You are the best. The very best actress in the world."

But right now, with Domenico looking at her as if she had just sprouted horns, Florence felt anything but the best. She felt rather like a heel.

"Samantha Day, eh?" Nonno said, as he autocratically waved the housekeeper out of the room, giving Florence just a small taste of how he must have acted before. "Yes, we really were alike, weren't we?"

Florence cringed. But in truth again she could only nod. "That's why I told you . . . your letter changed my life, Nonno. I had forgotten how to be myself. I was always acting in the role of Samantha Day and . . ." she looked up at Domenico, and with her eyes begging him to understand, said, "I had forgotten not only how to be myself but had forgotten . . . God."

But from the way Domenico's pulse pounded in his temple and the way his lips had turned almost white, Florence knew that he was mad, very mad, and that not telling him about Samantha Day sooner had been the wrong thing to do. She hadn't wanted Samantha Day to intrude in their relationship but, in spite of her desire, that was exactly what she was doing.

"You lied to me," Domenico ground out. "By omission, you lied." She gasped, but when his lips curled in recognition now of the famous sound as he finally understood why she had always seemed so familiar to him she wished that she could have prevented doing so. "Why? Why didn't you tell me?" he snarled out. "You knew I wondered at times if I had met you before or why you seemed so familiar to me. Why didn't you tell me?"

"I'm so sorry, Domenico. I see now that I should have, but I didn't want you to love Samantha Day the movie star," she blurted out the truth. "I wanted you to love me." She patted her chest. "Florence Celini."

He shook his head, and she cringed at the disgust she saw in his dark eyes. "I don't know who you are."

"But you see, I do now. I'm Florence Celini, the woman you have gotten to know while walking around this city. Who I have been while with you is who I actually am. The only thing I'm guilty of is not telling you about my professional life."

"You told me you own bookstores," he reminded her.

She had told him on their second day around the city. She had almost told him about being an actress then. She wished now that she had. "That's not a lie. I do. Several."

"You know, however, that they are secondary to your career as a world-famous movie star." He made a disgusted sound. "Most likely you own them at your accountant's advice. A tax break."

She couldn't honestly deny that, so she remained quiet.

"You have made a fool of me." He admitted to what really bothered him. "You have deceived me just like Giovanna did last year."

She shook her head back and forth, denying it. "Domenico . . . no. This is nothing like that. Giovanna acted falsely toward you because she wanted something from you — your name, wealth, social standing."

131

She motioned around the lavish *palazzo* in which they now sat. "Do I need any of that? Even with my own profession, I have all of that. Could I possibly be after you for any of what you might have? I don't know what your background is, but I seriously doubt that it could match mine."

"It does," Nonno spoke from her side. "Sorry, my dear. But Domenico's lineage is even older than our own and his *palazzo* makes this one seem like a small country home. Oh, and he's a duke, too."

She jumped out of her chair. "A duke!"

"We aren't royalty," Nonno grimaced. "We would have been had your father married the woman I wanted him to marry. . . ."

"A duke," she repeated and tapped her foot, something she did when about to make a point. "Wait a minute." She swiveled to face Domenico. "You're accusing me of not having told you about my career. What about your keeping being a duke from me?"

His lips curled in a very autocratic way, a very ducal way, actually. "Most women aren't upset when they discover I'm a duke."

"And do you think most men are upset to have Hollywood 'royalty' love them?"

Clapping his hands upon his thighs, Nonno stood suddenly and spoke. "I'm going to leave you two love birds to sort this out, but I think you two might want to 'wear' the virtues found in Colossians right now. To 'bear with each other and forgive whatever grievances you may have against one another,' might be a good thing, too." He started walking toward the door. "Oh," he turned back to them, "and I think I should tell you. It was *your* mother, Domenico, who I wanted my son, Cosimo, to marry. She would have made my family royal and . . . you would have been my grandson." He looked over at Florence and winked. "But for some reason I think he will soon be my grandson anyway. God really does have His way with us . . . if only we trust. . . ." He walked out of the room with laughter trailing behind him.

Florence looked at Domenico.

Domenico looked at her.

And before they even took another breath, they were in one another's arms; then their lips met in a kiss of forgiveness and love, which did indeed bind all the virtues of compassion, kindness, humility, gentleness, and patience together in perfect unity.

After a moment with the deep rumble of

a chuckle in his voice Domenico said, "Samantha Day, huh?"

"A duke, huh?" she replied.

And then they laughed, a glorious sound that filled the walls of the *palazzo* in exactly the way Florence's *babbo* had told her in his stories the palace always sounded.

It was the music of love.

And for the first time Samantha Day as Florence Celini was finally cast in a role that had a happy ending.

She didn't think she would ever want to star in any other.

Epilogue

One Year Later

Florence sat speechless when Domenico unveiled the huge painting he had bought for her. She gasped when *The Annunciation* by Fra Angelico, was before her. They had seen it together a year earlier when she had first come to Firenze to meet her *nonno*.

"I thought you had forgotten." He had told her the first time they had visited St. Marco's and seen the painting that he would buy a print of either it or the *Noli me Tangere* for her. She reached out to lightly touch its corner. "It's so beautiful. But . . . it isn't a print."

"No. That's why it took so long to get it for you. I had it specially commissioned by one of the foremost painters in Florence today."

"It looks just like the fresco. It's even the same size." She threw her arms around his neck. "I love it."

"And I love you."

Even though they had been married for six months now, Florence knew that she would never tire of hearing his wonderful voice speak those words to her. "It's the best present you could possibly give me. Especially now."

His eyes narrowed quizzically. "What do you mean, especially now?"

Reaching down she placed her hand over her flat tummy. "Because, dear husband, I have an 'announcement' to give to you. It might not be one along the same magnitude of that which the angel gave to Mary but —"

"We're going to have a child," he shouted out. It wasn't a question but a certainty.

She nodded. "In about eight months."

Tears came to his eyes. They didn't fall; they just made the dark orbs shine like jet. He pulled her close to him. "That is the best 'announcement,'" he said, chuckling, "you could ever give to me. I love you so much." He put his hand over her tummy and looked down at it with all the wonder of husbands throughout the ages who have longed to be fathers shining over his face. "Our child . . ." then, "But what about the movie? It's supposed to start shooting next week."

During the six months of their marriage she had been touched over and over again by how supportive he had been of her career. And the amazing thing was, now that she had shed the persona of Samantha Day and married her duke she had become even more sought after in Hollywood and for roles for which even her grandpop approved. The only problem was she didn't want to work as much anymore, especially now that a bambino was on the way. This movie was going to be the last she did for awhile. She wanted to spend time with her husband and child and *Nonno* and Grandpop. Her two grandfathers had become the best of friends and now that her grandpop had retired, he spent more time at the *palazzo* with them all than he did at his home in Texas.

"It will be fine. My part will be completed before I start to show, and after the babe is born, I'll take a break for awhile."

He nodded, accepting in his normal supportive way anything having to do with her work. "Who would have known?" he asked, after a dreamy moment of hugs and kisses and laughter.

"Known what?"

"What one letter asking for forgiveness could do. It started events that a year and a half later will even bring a new human into the world."

"Hmm," she agreed. "But it wasn't really just one letter, Darling. Along with *Nonno*'s, there was yours and Grandpop's notes, which in turn led me to my parents' letter, which then guided me to the letters from God." She looked over at the white Bible that her parents had given to her when she was a girl of seven. The binding was crinkly now and its pages a bit worn — a much "happier" Bible than a year earlier, when it had sat on her shelf forgotten and unused.

Seeing where her gaze was, Domenico reached for it. He opened it to her parent's letter. And he read:

To Florence, with love . . .

He turned his gaze away from that which they knew by heart and asked, "How could they have known?"

"Known?"

"That you would one day travel to Florence with love in your heart and not only heal a deep family wound but bring love to this Florentine man's heart?"

She smiled, that bright open happy smile for which Florence Celini-Ferretti was becoming well known. And putting her arms around her husband's shoulders, she said, "It's a God thing, my love. A God thing."

Dear Reader,

Living in Athens, Greece, with my family (husband, daughter, son, cat, and dog) one might think that a short trip to Florence would be easy. But it's been more than a year since I last visited the city.

But with the writing of this novella it was as if I was once again walking the streets of this amazing little city. But this time I visited it through the eyes of my character, Florence Celini. I stood with her when she first soaked in the view of this city of churches, and I was with her as she stood before Ghiberti's golden doors, and again while on the Ponte Vecchio looking out at the Arno River as it ran its timeless course to the sea far beyond. And it felt good, really good to be back in Firenze.

Real life for me is one of taking care of my family, getting together with friends, sitting at my desk weaving stories, going out and doing hands-on research, studying, praying, etc, etc. But in spite of all this I strive to keep my life as simple as possible. To make time to just be — to subtract the "busy-ness" — is one of my daily goals. Sometimes not attainable but still, much sought after!

I hope you enjoyed reading *To Florence with Love*. I delighted in writing it and as always, I thank God for His help in doing so. Without Him, I'm certain that I would still be on page one!

Many blessings to you!
Melanie Panagiotopoulos

Roman Holiday

by
Lois Richer

Prologue

"One day you'll wear my wedding dress, Dear."

Emily Cain let her fingers trail across the thick ivory satin one last time before refolding the delicate layers into the old cedar trunk. Maybe she would — one day. But until that happened, what was she to do with her life?

"God will light your path if you let Him, Emmy."

Her grandmother's words brought a sad little smile to Emily's lips. Dear Gran. How she missed that tiny woman and her snippets of encouragement. Especially now.

Two months ago Tad had called off their wedding and left town. The pain had eased a little since then. But what was she to do now? Emily couldn't help speculating on what was to become of her life.

"Be too busy for sin to overtake you."

Right now another of Gran's homilies sounded like very good advice. Emily closed the lid of the velvet-lined trunk, blocking the glossy sheen of bridal satin from view, just as she'd buried her hopes and dreams for the future. She shoved the trunk back into the closet, shut the door, then hurried out of the room. It was time to get on with her life.

But to do what?

Emily picked up the dog-eared syllabus off her desk and flipped through it. Perhaps it was time to return to her studies. She'd left college to be with Gran when the pneumonia had drained her tiny body, leaving her weak and needy. After the funeral, Tad proposed. Believing she would be moving as soon as they were married, Emily hadn't reenrolled.

The general arts courses held little interest now. Even the language studies her grandmother had encouraged seemed a useless waste of study. To whom would she speak Italian?

The doorbell rang, rousing her from wistful dreams.

"Special delivery, Miss. Sign here, please."

Emily signed for the letter, glancing at the return address. Nick Fellini. That name — Fellini. It seemed familiar, but she didn't know any Nick. She closed the door, slit the envelope, and tugged out a single sheet of paper.

My dear Miss Cain:

I extend to you sincere felicitations on the passing of your grandmother. I regret that only recently did we learn of her death, which, I'm sure, affects you deeply. I apologize for my tardy response. Though Mrs. Cain wrote to us some time ago, my own grandmother has been quite ill and has only recently recovered sufficiently to respond to Mrs. Cain's request.

In that regard, we would be pleased to have you visit us at your convenience. May I suggest you time your arrival soon to take advantage of our spring season, certainly the most beautiful time to see Rome? My grandmother is anxious to make the acquaintance of the namesake of her dear friend. Apparently some years ago, the two formed a pact to meet again, yet neither was able to keep the agreement. Perhaps you will visit instead?

In closing, may I encourage you to forward details of your journey as soon as possible. My grandmother dearly wishes to meet you.

Most sincerely,
Nick Fellini

Surprise and confusion vied for supremacy. *Go to Rome? Now?*

A longing flickered inside. To get away from here, just for awhile — if only she could. Emily reread the letter, pausing to reflect on each phrase, each undertone. His grandmother wanted her to visit, but what about this Nick? Did he live with her? He'd suggested she see Rome in the spring — which would be about now.

Apparently Gran had requested this family be her host, though she'd never told Emily of such a letter. But Gran had often mentioned her friend Cecelia, her Italian roommate for two years while she'd studied art in Rome. Cece Fellini. How many times had she noticed that name scratched on the thin blue sheets of airmail paper her grandmother had anticipated with such pleasure?

Emily trembled with excitement. *Italy.* She'd never been. But her entire childhood had been filled with Gran's stories about the eternal city. The fountains, the catacombs, the sculptures. Emily had spent her teenage years dreaming about the seven hills of Rome, imagined herself one day strolling through the Tivoli Gardens.

Perhaps a short trip would shed some light on the future, on her next step. There was nothing to hold her here. She'd quit her job when Tad said they'd be moving to Seattle and hadn't yet found new employment. Leaving now was no hardship. Escaping Chicago's slush and chilly spring winds would be wonderful.

Emily squeezed her eyes closed. *Is this my answer, Lord?*

If she was frugal, she could close up the apartment, travel for a few weeks, and return home refreshed, ready to focus on the future. Maybe then God would show her the next step. Emily inhaled deeply, her mind made up. A step of faith, Gran called it. She sat down to compose a telegram.

A week later, on a cold Midwest morning, Emily boarded the wide-body jet that would whisk her away from the past, to a city Gran had loved.

Chapter 1

"It's beyond anything I could ever have imagined." Emily whispered the words, unable to tear her eyes away from the window.

"Sì. Roma is a beautiful city." Nicolo Fellini seemed content to weave his way in and out of traffic while she stared.

"Is it always this busy?" Emily asked as the car zigged left, then right, in a crazy-quilt pattern that confused her sense of direction.

He nodded.

"Sì. Always. Many Americans have heard the saying that all roads lead to Rome. Perhaps this is true. Unfortunately, we have not so many roads to accommodate all those who arrive."

That short terse sentence didn't begin to answer the questions that bubbled inside her curious heart. In fact, it sounded as if Nick felt certain visitors should have stayed away! Emily wondered if she'd made a mistake coming here, believing they wanted her.

But surely a visit to Rome could never

be a mistake. She would just have to ignore Nick's grumpy attitude and savor every bit of pleasure from this trip.

As the car wound through an older, magnificently maintained suburb of the city, Emily pinched herself to make sure she was really here. Blossom-covered bougainvillea filled the air with perfume that danced on the breeze. Everywhere she looked it was green, lush, inviting. Expectation sent her stomach on a roller coaster ride as she peered ahead. The car turned into a circular driveway and stopped beneath a portico supported by white marble columns. The Fellinis lived in a villa?

And such a villa — small but exquisite. On either side of the entrance, flowers cascaded from baskets, burst from planters, and curved themselves up and over wrought-iron gates. To the right, behind the gates, a fountain cascaded sparkling water from a marble statue of a child holding an urn.

"*Bene.* This is the home of *mia nonna.* Welcome." Nick stood beside her open car door, waiting rather impatiently, if the truth were told.

Emily slid out of the car, absorbing her new surroundings.

"Your grandmother's home is lovely,"

she murmured, slightly unnerved by his compelling hand beneath her elbow. "You must love to share it with her."

He waited for her to precede him into the marble foyer, then stood silent, stern faced, as a young boy appeared with her two bags.

"To the blue room, Martino," he ordered.

The boy nodded, hurrying up the stairs. Suddenly the silence in the high-arched entry unnerved her. She was glad when Nick finally spoke, though the timbre of his words chilled her.

"It is my grandmother I love. Not her home, Miss Cain." He turned, motioning. "This way, please."

Emily opened her mouth to explain, then closed it. What was the point? For some unknown reason, he seemed determined to think the worst of her. But why was a mystery.

He marched down the corridor, stopped, pushed open a heavy door. The change in his tone amazed Emily.

"Nonna, I present to you Miss Emily Cain. Miss Cain, this is my grandmother, Cecelia Fellini."

A petite white-haired woman rose from her chair and held out her arms.

"*Buon pomeriggio!* Ah, my dear. It is so good to see you at last." She drew Emily into her arms and held on for a few moments, then gently moved her away, staring into her face as tears rolled down her cheeks. "*Mi scusi.* You have the look of your grandmother," she murmured softly. "I miss her yet."

Emily's heart spurted a warm tide of relief through her body. She'd been so afraid Mrs. Fellini would be stiff and formal, like her grandson. Instead she was warm, welcoming, every bit as lovely as Gran had said.

"It was very kind of you to invite me, Signora," she murmured in Italian.

"Bah! What is a visit between friends?" Mrs. Fellini waved a hand, indicating they should sit. "It is a time to enjoy each other. And you must call me Cece. Or Nonna, if you prefer."

One look at Nick's sour countenance told Emily all she needed to know about that suggestion. Fortunately he seemed to have little say in the matter.

"Gran spoke about you so often, I almost feel I know you. I would love to call you Cece, if you think it isn't improper." Emily sank onto the edge of a small velvet love seat, her gaze on the huge tray a woman placed in front of Cece.

"Cece is perfect. This wonderful woman is Maria. She has been with us many years. You must ask her if you need anything." Cece patted the woman's hand and waited till she'd smiled at Emily and pattered from the room before lifting her teacup. "Now we must have tea. I'm sure you are very tired from your flight."

She wasn't tired at all. Rather, Emily felt invigorated, eager to explore everything, all at once. But she accepted the cup of English tea and a delicate sandwich when offered by Nick and murmured her thanks. She didn't dare risk a glance at his face.

"I understand you were to be married, Miss Cain," he murmured as she took the first bite.

Emily almost choked. How dare he! She swallowed, setting her sandwich on the edge of her saucer.

"Yes, I was," she told him, glaring across the room. "Unfortunately things didn't work out."

"Ah."

What a wealth of condemnation could fill that simple word. Emily tamped down her irritation and concentrated on the tea.

"I, too, am so sorry about your broken engagement, Emily. It is a hard thing to endure, but sometimes it works out for the good." Cece's dark brown eyes conveyed her sympathy. A moment later they sparked with life.

"We must do everything we can to cheer her up, Nicolo. Which is why I have made a schedule." She reached into the pocket of her elegant linen dress and pulled out a sheet of paper. "You will have enough time this afternoon for a drive — just to get a feeling of the city. Roma is very beautiful in spring."

"I think it must be very beautiful all the time, but —"

"I'm sorry, Nonna, but I will not be available to escort Miss Cain today."

Not ever, if Emily understood the frost in his voice.

"But I had planned —"

"*Scusi, per favore*, Signor, Signora." Emily shifted uncomfortably when both heads turned toward her, but nothing could stem the words she felt compelled to say. "I never expected anyone to take time off to show me around. In fact, I'm looking forward to exploring Rome on my own. Please don't alter your routines for me."

Nick looked relieved. Cece looked put out.

"But I so wanted you two to get to know each other."

"I have my classes, Nonna. You know that." Nick set down his cup. "In fact, I must be off even now." He turned toward Emily, executed a slight bow, his face implacable. "Maria will show you to your room. Please feel welcome. Arrivederci." Then he walked out of the room. A second later the front door thudded closed.

"Please to excuse Nicolo." Cece's alabaster skin wrinkled in a frown. "He does not mean to be rude. He has much to do at his school."

"He's still going to school?" Emily blinked, trying to imagine Nick at her college.

Cece burst into delighted giggles. "No, no, my dear. He is a professor. Of history. His classes are most sought after and always he tries to make them interesting for his students. Nicolo is very serious about his school."

"I see." Emily listened to her chitchat as she sipped the tea and munched on sandwiches. Fifteen minutes later Maria returned. Emily decided it was now or never.

"I am sure la signora should rest for awhile, Maria. And while she does, I shall hire a taxi to take me on a tour. Per favore, would you show me the telephone?"

In rapid fire Italian, Maria tossed away the taxi idea and offered her grandson as a chauffeur. Twenty minutes later Emily was seated beside Martino and they were rushing toward the center of the city.

"So you are *la fidanzata*," he said loudly, grinding gears so she could get a better look at the Colosseum.

Emily frowned, searched her vocabulary. Fiancée?

"Oh, no," she gasped, her cheeks burning with embarrassment. "You must have me mixed up with someone else. I'm just visiting."

Martino grinned, his white teeth flashing in the sun.

"Oh, no, I hear," he told her in labored English. "La signora says the *fidanzata* of Signor Nicolo arrives today."

He slammed on the brakes, screamed something in rapid Italian, then zipped them back into traffic. Emily had no time to be frightened. Besides, in the back of her mind, she was remembering a comment her grandmother had made long ago.

"Cece and I promised each other we'd get our children together, watch them fall in love, and be doting grandmothers."

Was that why Signora Fellini had invited Emily to Rome? As a prospective bride for her grandson?

A light clicked on inside her brain.

No wonder Nick seemed hostile!

Chapter 2

"Welcome to the Piazza di Spagna — the so-called Spanish steps, which lead to the Church of Trinita dei Monti," Nick waved a hand. "I'm sure you can't help but notice the azaleas. It is a springtime tradition in Rome to decorate the steps with them. If you'd like to take a break, we will gather together at the top in fifteen minutes to discuss the obelisk."

He couldn't help but notice her sitting there.

The polished gold of Emily Cain's long hair spun round her shoulders like a cape as she peered at the book in her lap. Her clothes were not the pricey designer brands of the American students who'd paid to attend his lecture series. She wore a simple green skirt that brushed her ankles, a sleeveless cotton top of pale pink that matched the flowers in her skirt, and a pair of open-toed sandals. Yet she looked like a queen holding court.

Was that what irritated him whenever he looked at her — - her demeanor? How petty was that?

Nick climbed the steps to where she sat framed by the azaleas.

"*Ciao*," he murmured.

She glanced up, her green eyes wide with surprise. A moment later the light dimmed.

"Oh, hello." She thrust one finger in her book, then closed it. Though her gaze remained on him, she volunteered nothing further.

"Are you having a good day of sightseeing?" he asked, wishing he hadn't bothered her. But that would have been churlish, and only this morning he'd promised Nonna he would be kinder to Miss Cain.

"Lovely."

Clearly she intended to volunteer nothing. In fact, her whole body had stiffened, as if prepared to repel him. A pinch of regret flicked his conscience. He deserved her ire. She'd done nothing to merit the brunt of his anger. Nothing but accept his grandmother's invitation to come here.

"Why are you here, Nick?"

The question surprised him.

"What do you mean?"

She waved a hand. "I'm sure there's nothing here that you haven't seen before. Why are you here?"

"I have a class of students. From America, actually. I make it a point for them to get out of the tour bus and climb the steps, to relax a bit before we continue with our studies." Did she suspect him of following her?

"Where are they now?" She glanced around.

He pointed. "No one can come to Piazza di Spagna and not enjoy a cup of —" he frowned, pretended to search for the English word.

"Cappuccino?" she supplied.

He nodded, then realized it had not been the right thing to say. Emily Cain was not enjoying such a treat. In fact, as far as he could ascertain from his grandmother, she was on a very strict budget. Which was another reason he'd avoided her. He felt guilty every time he looked at her.

"Would you like one?" he offered belatedly.

She wrinkled her nose, then shook her head, blond hair dancing in the sunlight.

"No, thanks. I had one the other day. It's too strong. I prefer my water." She pointed to the bag near her feet, then glanced back up the steps, her gaze wistful.

"You have already been up there?"

The blond hair danced its little jig once

more as she shook her head.

"Oh, but this is necessary." He glanced upward, unable to stem the words that came so naturally. "The church of Trinita dei Monti was built in 1495 for the use of French Catholics. Today it houses a most famous fresco entitled *Descent from the Cross*."

"I know."

"But you will not go there?" Something was wrong and he didn't understand what it was. Concern flooded him. "Are you all right?"

"Not really." She did glance up at him then. Her green eyes were turbulent with unspoken emotion. "I've just come from the Colosseum. It — bothered me."

"Ah." This, at least, Nick understood. He sank down on the step beside her. "The atmosphere can be a little over-whelming."

"Overwhelming?" She tipped up her head, her eyes blazing. "It's — disgusting!" She swallowed, but her chin remained thrust out. "I suppose it's not nice to say such a thing to you, since this is your country, but I can't help it. Feeding people to lions for their beliefs — it's barbaric."

"Yes, it is. But some historians do not believe that is true, Emily," he murmured

162

gently. "Though, of course, no one can say for sure. We do know that the *Ludi Circenses* became favorite shows of the Romans because they were invented to develop the war-like spirit that made Romans the conquerors of the world. This is the origin of the gladiators — professionals trained to fight to the death against many wild animals."

He paused, gauged her response as interested, then continued.

"In the early fifth century, a monk named Telemachus, who had come from the east, one day entered the arena and tried to place himself between the gladiators while he begged the people to stop the horrible shows. The people protested, in fact, they stoned him to death. But from that day, the shows ended."

Emily sat silent while she considered his comments.

"Perhaps," she sighed. "I don't know. But I do know that Christians died for their faith. Many of them in Rome. Your talk of stoning makes me think of Stephen. He prayed, at the end. Do you remember?" She cocked her head like a curious bird. "How could he forgive them? How could he?"

Nick knew his class waited, that he had

to go. But how could he leave Emily like this? Something more than the deaths of the early Christians bothered her.

"It isn't easy to understand," he murmured. "But many of those who died were men and women who knew Jesus, who'd lived with Him, talked to Him. Perhaps they felt it was worth anything to be with Him again."

"Perhaps." She stared at him, her green eyes swirling with glints of something he couldn't understand.

"I must go now." Nick rose, dusting the seat of his pants. "My class, you understand. I promised them a full day."

He stood there, looking down at her, loathe to leave, but afraid to stay. Something about her outburst had touched him, in spite of his resolve not to get involved. Emily Cain was turning out to be anything but the spoiled brat he'd expected.

She smiled, not the radiant one he'd glimpsed before. This was merely a polite tipping of her lips.

"Thanks for stopping. I guess I'd better get on, too." She rose, stowed her book inside her bag and slung the handle over one shoulder. "Perhaps I'll see you at dinner. Good-bye."

"*Ciao*, Emily."

She smiled a real smile then. "Ciao," she repeated, then danced down the steps where she paused to study the Fountain of the Barcaccia by Bernini for a few short minutes before veering right into the Piazza Mignanelli.

Nick found himself hoping she'd stop in front of the Progaganda Fide Palace to study the column of the Immaculate Conception. For some reason he wanted her to see all of Rome's history, not just the ugly parts. Though why that should matter to him wasn't immediately clear.

He had no intention of marrying anyone, let alone Emily Cain, no matter how high his Nonna's hopes. Alexandra's death three years ago had taught him that hard lesson. He'd accepted that love, marriage, and the family that inevitably went with it were not to be his.

Which was why he'd chosen the orphanage and the children.

At least while he was with them, he didn't feel so alone.

Chapter 3

Today would have been her wedding day, if Tad hadn't deserted her.

Emily slipped from her room and padded down the staircase to the front door, her bag with its full water bottle slung over one shoulder. The taxi she'd called for waited outside. She climbed in quickly, giving her directions. Thankfully, traffic was still light, as light as traffic here ever got, and she arrived at the Vatican in good time, well before Nick.

He didn't know she would be there, of course. She'd revealed her plans to no one. But last night, after she'd heard him tell Maria he had to leave early to take his students through the Papal Palace and would not be in for dinner, she'd made her decision.

She'd been in Rome for a week. Hopping on and off the trundling shuttle buses that offered headphones and an ongoing tour of the highlights every tourist should see had become a simple matter.

But it wasn't enough. Emily found herself longing to know more about the early church, about its founders and their deep commitment to a faith that willingly gave up family and friends, even life.

Today, as she watched young lovers linger beside fountains, she thought about Tad. How could he have dumped her like that — without warning? Had he ever loved her? Though she'd tried to pretend otherwise, Emily was well aware of the kernel of bitterness that lodged deep inside her heart and stopped her from forgiving him. Maybe if she could understand how others had handled betrayal, she would understand how God could have let this happen to her.

Nick Fellini was a bottomless pit of knowledge. She'd heard him yesterday when she'd been sipping her water and admiring the elegant hotels and coffeehouses on the Via Vittorio Veneto. She'd been so intrigued by his comments about Bernini's fountain of the Bees, that she'd tagged along to listen to him speak about the Capuchin Church. She'd even accompanied his group as they visited the Baths of Diocletian. Her nervousness about being seen had disappeared the longer he spoke. He had a knack of bringing the past alive, of drawing word pictures that helped her visualize Rome's history in Technicolor.

"I see you intend to accompany us again today." Nick stood behind her, his mouth drawn in a tight line.

Emily flushed.

"I don't want to bother you," she murmured, praying he'd let her stay. "Really I don't. And I've tried to keep out of your way. But you are so knowledgeable about everything. Listening to you is far better than trying to decipher those headphones."

He blinked, then a crooked smile pulled up the corners of his mouth.

"I guess one might take that for flattery."

"Oh, I wasn't flattering you. It's the truth. I learned so much about the baths yesterday. Why don't they put those details in the books?" Emily saw the group of students beyond him, and realized they were waiting. "I'm sorry, I've kept you from your work. But would it really be too much to allow me to tag along? I promise I won't get in the way or ask any questions. I just want to learn."

"I noticed how intent you were yesterday. Our history seems important to you. Why is that?" he asked, his frown rippling his smooth olive forehead.

Emily knew her cheeks were red, but she didn't look away from his scrutiny.

"I want to understand how the first church grew and developed. Besides," she grinned, "If I'm hanging around with your group, you won't have to keep sidestepping your grandmother's questions about showing me the city."

It was probably the wrong thing to say. His already dark eyes deepened to bittersweet-chocolate. But after a moment, he tossed back his curly head and chuckled.

"Tag along for as much of the tour as you can tolerate, Emily Cain. I hope you find the answers you look for." He turned to the group. "Is everyone ready? Then — *Benvenuto a Piazza San Pietro*. Welcome to St. Peter's Square."

The morning was filled with wonder for Emily as Nick explained the history behind the Vatican, beginning with the Egyptian obelisk in the center of the square. Centuries before people just like her had created and inscribed this stone. Amazing!

"We move now to take a better look at the Porta Santa, the Holy Door. It is opened only every twenty-five years, on Christmas Eve." Nick continued his descriptions, leading them through the Vatican's splendor while he drew graphic images of days gone by.

Tantalized by his recounting, Emily

found herself weeping as he described the apostle Peter's death and his wish to be crucified upside down because he wasn't worthy to die as Christ had. How, she wondered, as she stared at the celebrated bronze statue of St. Peter, how could he have forgiven his Roman persecutors when she couldn't forgive Tad for making a mistake?

It seemed only minutes until the tour was completed and the rest of the students departed on a bus for a field trip. Freed of their chatter and with plenty of time left, Emily wandered back through the basilica until she stood in the first chapel of the right aisle and once more beheld Michelangelo's *Pietà*.

"I thought perhaps I'd find you here." Nick's quiet voice sounded neither impatient nor irritated.

"You did?" Emily twisted to peer into his face. "Why?"

He nodded and returned his gaze to the statue.

"I noticed earlier that you seemed drawn to this work. More so than many of my students. What particularly attracts you?"

"It doesn't attract me," she murmured, staring at the marble Mary holding her dead son. "It — puzzles me, confuses me.

Mostly it makes me angry. Why isn't she upset? Why does she look so — resigned? I just can't figure it out."

"Well, if you're looking to understand grace, I'm not sure anyone can." He tilted back on his heels, surveying the marble. "Grace, true grace, is freely granted, without strings. Perhaps that's why the artist chiseled her head bowed in that manner. She accepted God's will when she first heard Gabriel's words, continued to accept it, even though it cost her a son. I believe she realized that the price outweighed her sacrifice."

"Perhaps." Suddenly Emily wanted to be outside, to feel the warmth of the sun on her skin, to smell the flowers and forget about Tad and everything that could have been. "You don't have to stay," she told Nick. "I don't want to take up your afternoon. Thank you for letting me listen to the lecture."

She turned and walked through the basilica and out the door, shame nipping at her as she realized how close she was to tears. Angrily she scrubbed her eyes, drawing in deep breaths of control. Nicolo Fellini didn't need to hear about her petty disappointments.

"As it happens, I'm free this afternoon.

Would you like to share lunch with me?" He matched her step for step until Emily reached the avenue.

"Look," Emily muttered, twisting to glare at him. He felt sorry for her, and she didn't want that. "You've made it more than obvious that you have no desire to shunt me around Rome. Fine. I'm happy to potter about on my own, anyway. You can go on back to your college, or wherever you disappear to each night, with a clear conscience."

His eyes widened. "Where I disappear —"

"I've seen you slip out when you think your grandmother is safely tucked up in her room. I've heard you come back, sometimes after midnight." She saw the color leave his cheeks and wondered what he was doing in those hours. "Don't worry, I haven't said anything. It's none of my business who you hang out with."

Nick's forehead furrowed, but his gaze never left hers. Finally he huffed out a huge sigh.

"I'm sorry, Emily. I owe you an apology. This situation is not of your creating. I've been rude and ungracious, and my grandmother would tear a strip off me if she knew. This is not how she raised her grandson to behave."

"Your grandmother raised you?" That explained the bond between them.

"We can't stand on the street talking." He stepped out of the way of a group of schoolgirls in navy-and-white uniforms and waited until they'd passed. "Let me buy you lunch. I know the perfect *trattoria*."

In less than five minutes Nick had maneuvered her down a tiny street and seated her at a table that offered a perfect view of the Vatican.

"May I order for you? I promise you will like their food." His dark eyes sparkled with excitement. Emily could do little but nod and listen as he conversed with their waiter in Italian too rapid for her to follow.

"So, shortly our meal will arrive." He took a sip of his cappuccino. "Where were we?"

"You were telling me that your grandmother raised you." For the first time Emily felt a connection with Nick as he described his parents' death in a plane crash when he was just eight. "I was a very active child," he admitted. "But Nonna never tried to hold me back or keep me from trying things. I had a wonderful childhood."

"I'm glad. It's rather like my story," she murmured, remembering the short months after her mother had died when her father seemed to lose his own will to battle the cancer filling his body. "I was older than you, a very angry teen. But Gran was patient, and we got along famously. I still miss her."

"I'm sure." He reached across the table and squeezed her fingers. "How sad to lose everyone you love. I don't know what I shall do when —" The unspoken words hung between them.

"Perhaps you'll be married with your own family by then," she offered quietly, trying to imagine stiff and formal Nick unbending enough to play with his own children. The image did not compute.

"I shall never marry."

Emily stared. He sounded so certain. She opened her mouth to ask why and then realized that would be prying. But he saw her reaction and smiled, albeit a sad, tired smile.

"Sooner or later my grandmother will tell you. I suppose I might as well give you my version first." He sighed, staring down the street. "Three years ago I was engaged to be married. But before the wedding could take place, *ma fidanzata* was injured in a car accident. She died later."

"Oh, but surely, given enough time, you'll meet someone else. . . ." The words died a silent death when she saw his head shake.

"I don't believe God intends for me to marry." He glanced at her, lips curved in a wry smile. "Hence my sour attitude. My *nonna* wishes to keep her pact with your grandmother and would have the two of us marry immediately."

"Yes, I'd heard something about that plan from Martino." She smiled, trying to show she hadn't taken it seriously. "But if that was your fear, you needn't have worried. I'm not prepared to be engaged to anyone. Once was more than enough."

Nick waited until the waiter had set steaming bowls of pasta redolent with robust tomato sauce, spicy peppers, and fresh basil before them. Once the basket of rolls was in place and the waiter had left, he asked the question she didn't want to answer.

"What happened to your bridegroom?"

Emily lifted her fork and pushed at the thick noodles, her appetite diminished.

"He left." She glanced up, saw the questions in his expressive eyes and sighed. Might as well get it over with. "He claimed he didn't love me, that he'd made a mistake. And then he called it off. As a matter of fact, today would have been our wedding day."

"I'm so sorry, *Carissa*. But surely you are relieved that this happened —"

Emily held up her hand.

"Please don't say it's for the best, or it would have been worse if he'd found out later. I've heard it all a thousand times before, told myself the same things." She felt the bitterness creep into her voice. "It doesn't help much."

"This feeling, I know it well." He grinned. "Smashing something, that would help, sì? Perhaps the urn of flowers would soothe the sting."

She giggled.

"Well, I don't know that I'd go that far. But I do get ticked that he didn't think it through before he proposed and I'd made all those plans."

"Ticked?" Nick frowned. "I do not know this word."

"Angry. Upset. Frustrated."

"Quanti anni hai, Emily?" How old are you?

"Twenty-two. What's that got to do with it?" She bit into her pasta and found it surpassed anything she'd ever tasted. "Does it

176

hurt any less if you get dumped when you're older?"

"No. But you are very young. You have time to meet other people, to choose what you will do with your life. Marriage is not all there is."

"This coming from an Italian," she teased, but her smile quickly drooped. "That's just it, don't you see? I thought I had my life mapped out, that I knew where God wanted me. Now everything is all upset and I haven't the faintest idea where to go from here. This is a lovely holiday and I'm grateful for it," she hurried on, anxious to make him understand. "But after it's over and I'm back at home — then what do I do?"

"I don't know. But I don't think it is a problem for God. He will reveal His wishes at the right time. It's the waiting that is so difficult." He tasted his own meal.

They put all conversation on hold as they ate, savoring each bite of this most Italian of meals. At last Nick pushed away his empty dish, stretched out his arms.

"No one knows the future, Emily. But in the meantime, you are in Roma. That is not too hard to bear, is it?"

"No." As she stared into his handsome face, Emily realized that being here wasn't a hardship at all. Nick was good company, someday he might even be a friend. And when she was back in Chicago, she would take out the memory of these days and be glad she'd been able to experience this eternal city.

"So what shall we do this afternoon? I am at your disposal until this evening."

"And then what?" she asked, knowing that this was one of the nights he disappeared. "Have you something special planned for this evening?"

"Just some work," he told her, but he kept his face averted, pretending to fiddle with his chair. "Are you ready to go?"

"Go where?" Emily rose, anticipation rising in spite of herself.

"I think it is time to broaden your horizons, Miss Cain. We shall visit the forum."

As she'd deliberately left this visit off her previous itinerary, hoping to arrange a personal tour, Emily could barely contain her excitement.

"And will you explain it all to me?" she demanded. "Every detail? You won't leave anything out?"

Nick laughed, looped her arm through his, and led her down the street.

"This is a dangerous thing to say to an historian, Emily. I promise I will regale you with so many details that you will beg me to be quiet."

Emily hid her smile as she walked beside him, aware of the curious glances they drew. She still didn't understand what God had planned for her, but an afternoon at the forum was a perfect way to wait. Especially when Nick was in such a jolly mood.

Maybe they would become good friends.

Someday.

Chapter 4

Nick slipped into his grandmother's villa, trying to cause as little noise as possible. It was late enough that everyone should be asleep, but just in case, he took off his shoes before climbing the stairs, trying to ensure the taped gauze pad stayed in place until he reached his own bathroom. He almost made it.

But he'd forgotten the big urn his grandmother had recently ordered to be placed outside Emily's door and filled with the fragrant pink roses grown in the villa's gardens.

"Ow!" he yelped, then swallowed the rest of his words as pain radiated from his big toe, up his leg. One shoe clunked to the floor, cracking through the silent house like thunder on a stormy night.

Unfortunately, Emily's door opened before he could get inside his room.

"Nick? What's the matter?" She was swathed from neck to tiptoe in a sprigged cotton robe tied securely around her waist. Her trademark blond hair cascaded over her narrow shoulders. She immediately saw his injury. "What happened?"

"Just a scratch. Nothing more." He tried to hold the saturated gauze in place, but a trickle of blood betrayed him.

"A scratch doesn't bleed like that." She glanced around the landing, then pointed to the staircase. "Let's go to the kitchen so we don't disturb your grandmother. I'll clean that for you."

"It doesn't matter. I can do it." Frustrated by his inability to stop the bleeding, he grabbed his handkerchief and wrapped it around his arm, realizing he'd reopened the cut.

"Go downstairs or I will alert your grandmother about your injury at breakfast tomorrow," Emily ordered, the light of battle gleaming in her emerald eyes.

Nick glared at her, assessing her intent as he studied her freshly scrubbed face. She meant it. But if Emily told Nonna, she'd insist on knowing where he'd received the injury. He couldn't lie to his grandmother. Even if she didn't know immediately, and she would, he'd never lied to her in all these years. He'd have to explain. Then the truth about his clandestine activities would be out. He didn't want that.

"All right." He nodded, motioning for her to go first. "On one condition. You tell my grandmother nothing about this."

Emily stopped so abruptly, he almost bumped into her. She twisted, stared at him, a frown marring the smoothness of her forehead.

"Is it something bad? Are you in trouble?"

"No, of course not." He motioned for her to go, then followed her into the kitchen. Once she'd flicked the light on, he moved to the sink and lifted the first-aid kit from under the counter before removing the gauze pad and throwing it in the garbage. Perhaps if she kept busy, she'd forget her questions.

"Oh, my goodness! What did you do?" Emily didn't wait for his response, but removed a sterile pad and immediately began swabbing the area with antiseptic cleaner.

"I was trying to fix something. The tool slipped and . . ." He shrugged.

"I think, for your own health, you might consider hiring someone to do whatever repairs you require. History seems more your forte." She grinned at him, obviously enjoying the flush of red that burned his cheeks.

"You're calling me an — what is the term? Egghead?" It was fun to joke and tease with someone. The evening visits he made three times a week sometimes left him awake for hours afterward, wondering why there wasn't more he could do.

"A very knowledgeable egghead," she murmured, then bit her bottom lip in concentration as she pressed the plasters holding his bandage into place. "But not, I think, about tools. Is that too tight? Have I made it worse?"

"It's fine. Thank you." He flexed his hand, felt relief that the stiffness was abating already. "I'm glad you insisted on doing this, Emily. I don't know how I would have managed with one hand. Where did you learn to dress wounds?"

"I nursed Gran a lot." Emily rinsed the sink and washed down the counters as she spoke. "Sometimes she was a bit awkward, because of her walking stick, and would injure herself." Her voice dropped and he knew she was remembering. "I got a lot of practice patching her up, but I never minded. It was the least I could do." She turned off the tap, wiped the sink dry, and hung up the towel. "Well, if there's nothing else?"

He didn't want to leave her, not yet. He

wanted her to stay, to talk to him. Which was not a good idea. He ignored his brain's warning.

"Could you put on the kettle?" he asked quietly. "I think I'd like a cup of tea. Suddenly I'm wide awake."

"Of course." She moved around the kitchen easily as if she'd been in here, done this a hundred times before. Perhaps she had.

Nick was ashamed to realize he'd never wondered what Emily did with her evenings. His pulse did a double step as he imagined her with the children. How would she handle them? Did she like children?

"Where do you go after dinner?" she asked, lifting the teapot from the shelf where Maria kept it. "It's quite late by the time we finish dinner."

"Quite late?" He blinked, then realized that she probably did find their dinner hour unusual. "What time do you eat dinner in Chicago?"

"Around six. Seven if I'm really late." She held up two tea choices and waited till he'd pointed at one. "Earl Grey. I might have known."

"Is there something wrong with this tea?"

She giggled at him.

"Of course not. I've had it quite often." She swished boiling water into the pot, let it heat the china, then dumped it out and refilled the delicate blue pot. "How do you say 'herb tea' in Italian?"

He stared at her shining swath of hair, while his mind worked to decipher her meaning.

"Herb? This is a name for another kind of tea? Named for a famous person perhaps?"

Emily's giggles echoed around the old stone kitchen, brightening the terra-cotta walls and sending a shaft of warmth through him.

"What is funny?" he asked, enjoying the sight of her beautiful face glowing pinkly from her extended afternoon in the sun. Her jade eyes sparkled and danced with mirth.

"You are. Herb tea," she repeated. "Herbs. You know, like parsley and peppermint, sage and basil. Herbs. You make tea out of them."

"You are telling me that Americans drink basil tea?" He screwed up his face. "I do not think you will find such a thing in Rome, Emily."

"Spice." She tried again. "How about orange spice tea?"

He shook his head. "I don't know about this tea. I will have to ask Maria. Perhaps she will take you to the market and you may find it there." He picked up the teapot in his good hand. "Shall we drink this ordinary tea on the patio?"

"Oh, yes, please." Emily placed two cups, the sugar bowl, and a spoon on a tray and carried them out to the little wrought-iron table that sat just beyond the kitchen door. "This is the most wonderful place at night. Look at that sky. Inky black." She set the tray down and tilted her head back to stare upward. "So beautiful," she whispered.

He wanted to agree, but it wasn't the sky he was looking at, it was she. Here in the garden, with only the fountain light to illuminate, she resembled one of Michelangelo's sculptures. Her blond hair cascaded over her shoulders and down her back like spun gold, her pure clear profile as beautiful as any finely sculpted marble in all of Rome.

Then she spun around on her toes, and the mirage was broken. She wasn't chilly marble on display, never to be touched. Emily was real, alive. She plopped down into her chair and poured the tea.

"Are you going to tell me where you

were tonight or not?" she demanded, thrusting a steaming cup toward him.

"Not," Nick answered quickly. Too quickly. One golden eyebrow arched upward.

"Why? Is it a secret?"

"No." He busied himself sipping his tea, wishing he could think of a way to avoid her questions. She looked small and delicate, but he was beginning to realize that quiet beauty only served to hide her resolve and tenaciousness.

"I don't think you return to your school," she murmured, her eyes fixed on the fountain beyond as she mused on the problem. "Who would go there at night when there are so many sights to see in the city by starlight?" She twisted around, surveying him once more. "But if you were chauffeuring students to see the sights, how did you hurt yourself? Did your car break down?"

Amused by her mistaken deductions, Nick contented himself with studying the view in his grandmother's garden, including the woman across from him.

"You're not going to tell me?" she asked when she'd run out of *what ifs*.

"And ruin your fun?" He shook his head. "No. I won't do that."

"Then I shall have to find out for myself. Good night."

Before he'd managed to scramble to his feet, she'd pranced across the flagstones and inside the house, her long housecoat flapping at her legs.

"Good night," he murmured, knowing she wouldn't hear him.

He sat in the garden a long time, thinking, dreaming of something he'd never have. At last he rose, gathered up the tea things, and took them to the kitchen.

But by the time he was lying in bed, Nick had come to only one conclusion. He'd have to be very careful when next he left the villa for a visit.

Emily kept to the shadows as she followed Nick's tall figure down the darkened street two nights later. A sense of unease tiptoed up her spine, but she refused to acknowledge it. This was a section of Rome she'd never visited, but she needed no guidebook to tell her it was a slum. These old buildings had no one lovingly restoring their finish. Cracked windows, peeling walls, and uneven walkways broadcast that few people cared what happened in this neighborhood.

It was such a change from Cece's neighborhood and from the carefully maintained tourist sights. What was Nick doing here?

She stopped, suddenly realizing that he'd disappeared. The taxi driver had warned her to be careful, but he was long gone and now she was alone. She had to keep going.

"Curiosity killed the cat," Gran had often reminded her. Emily refused to dwell on that.

"Where did he go?" she muttered, edging past another storefront. Two men ogled her. Suddenly the sound of children's voices drew her on. She walked quickly toward the sound and soon arrived at a doorway, opened wide to let in a night breeze.

Conscious that the two men had followed her, Emily slipped inside and moved to one corner, behind a plant, certain that this must be the place Nick disappeared to so often.

The walls had been whitewashed over patches of peeling plaster that, in spite of the garish light from overhead fluorescent lights, lent a fresh clean appearance to the inside of the old building. The stone floor bore more than its share of cracks, nicks, and dents, but it was clean and tidy. A long table ran almost the entire length of the front room with benches on either side.

As Emily stared, children poured in through a door in the rear, wiggling and jiggling into their seats with giggles that echoed against the high ceiling and tumbled back down on their black shiny heads. Though obviously poor, evidenced by tattered clothing that drooped off the shoulders of most of them, none of the children seemed unhappy. They folded their hands, bowed their heads, and quietly waited while a tall woman with white hair said grace, then eagerly awaited their bowl full of what looked to be stew.

So engrossed was she in them that she failed to notice someone had discovered her.

"Come si chiama?" What is your name?

Emily jerked to attention, bumped her forehead on the huge azalea bush and blinked the tiny boy before her into view.

"Ah, Emily," she mumbled, without thinking.

"Piacere di conoscerla."

So the little sprite was pleased to see her. Emily grinned, hunkered down, and held out one hand and asked him his name.

"Mario," she repeated. *"Ma, dove abiti?"*

He stared at her as if she were slightly addlepated, then motioned around him. Here, she realized. Mario lived here.

"Buon compleanno, Mario." Nick's voice echoed around the room.

"Grazie!" Mario was all smiles, even favoring the crowd with a little bow.

It was the child's birthday? Realizing that all eyes were also upon her, Emily slipped from her hiding place and repeated the congratulations, which Mario graciously accepted. He then wrapped his hand around her arm and pulled until she was forced to follow him to Nick who then introduced her to the entire assembly. The children greeted her, then turned back to devour their food. Several moments later another woman carried in a huge birthday cake, which she placed in front of Mario while everyone sang to him.

"I might have known you'd follow me."

"What is this place?" she whispered to Nick, hoping he wouldn't chastise her here, in front of everyone. "An orphanage?"

"Sort of. More like a mission. *La Dolce Vita.* The good sisters try to give these children a home, a school, and some much-needed mothering." He paused, then glanced down at her. "I help out whenever I can."

She opened her mouth, but a loud clapping stopped her response. One of the sis-

191

ters told the group Mario would now receive his birthday gift. From behind a door she wheeled a very old bicycle that had been cleaned and polished as much as it would stand. Mario's brown eyes grew even larger, and he didn't move until one of the children pushed him forward.

Reverently he touched the handlebars, accepting the bike with several murmured *grazie*'s. At everyone's urging he climbed on and pedaled furiously until Nick stopped him and suggested he try it outside in the yard. Everyone rushed to watch. Emily moved to follow, but Nick's hand on her arm stopped her. She glanced up, surprised by the frown on his face.

"Why are you here? Did my grandmother send you?"

"No. I told you I would find out where you disappear to at night. But I never expected this. I wish you'd told me." She thought of the many evenings she'd spent alone, lonely for the sound of another human voice. She could have come here, shared this.

"You do?" He frowned. "Why?"

"Because I would have enjoyed coming. I love kids."

"You must go now, Emily. It isn't safe here at night." His dark eyes flashed with temper. "I wish you hadn't come here."

"But I did. And if it's so dangerous, then I can't go home by myself, can I?" She began stacking the dishes. "So I'll leave when you do. In the meantime, I can help." Suddenly his injury made sense. "You were fixing that bike, weren't you? That's how you hurt yourself."

His expression didn't change, but Emily caught the flicker through his eyes and knew she was right. He'd been working on a birthday gift for Mario.

"Why don't you serve the sisters their coffee outside while I deal with these? I'm sure they'd appreciate a break," she murmured, her heart swelling.

He looked about to argue, then shrugged and walked through the rear door. Above the sink was a huge window, open to the evening. As she scrubbed and scoured, Emily could both see and hear the children dashing about in a series of games. She'd almost finished the last dish by the time they all trooped back in to enjoy Mario's cake.

"You didn't have to do that." Nick peered down at her, eyes fixed on her reddened hands. "The sisters didn't expect it."

"Of course they didn't. I just wanted to

help. What happens now? They seem far too excited to sleep. Where do they sleep, by the way?" She glanced around, reminded that the building had looked too narrow from the outside to offer enough space for beds for everyone.

"They sleep upstairs." He took her arm. "Come on. This is a special time. Everyone listens while one of the sisters tells a story."

Curious, Emily walked beside him into the room where they'd eaten. Now the benches were pushed under the table, and the children were sitting cross-legged on what looked like old quilts. Nick guided her to a seat, but before they could sit down, the older of the sisters approached them and whispered in Nick's ear.

"She'd like to know if you'd tell them a Bible story." He studied her face. "You can say no if you want to. I'll tell her your Italian isn't up to it."

"Actually I–I'd like to. If you think my Italian is up to it. I used to have a Sunday school class. They remind me of it." She held her breath, waiting for his approval, then wondered why it seemed so important to tell a story. One glance at the children's shining faces told her why. For them.

"There's nothing wrong with your

Italian, but even if there were, they'd just laugh. They love stories and visitors." Nick squinted. "You're sure?"

She nodded and a few minutes later she, too, sat cross-legged, surrounded by the children. Mario had managed to assume the pride of position at her left side, and he shushed the group before grinning at her.

The only story that came to mind was the one about Noah, and she was a little hesitant to name animals she couldn't describe. Gran was right, vocabulary lessons were more important than she'd ever imagined. Still, it was thanks to Gran that she was able to speak to these little ones at all.

When Sister glanced at her watch, Emily quickly concluded the story and thanked them for listening. Mario reached out and shook her hand with his little one, his smile spread across his face.

"*Mi dispiace, ma non parlo l'italiano molto bene.* Sorry, I don't speak Italian well," she apologized.

"*Non fa niente. La capisco benissimo.* That's all right. I understand you very well." Mario thanked her for coming to his birthday party. Then, en masse, the group wished her *buona sera.*

"Come. We must leave now. Some tired children need their rest." Nick offered a hand to draw her to her feet, then waved at the children. *Buona notte.* "Good night."

Amidst the responses, he quickly ushered her out of the building and down the street to his car. Once inside they sped away, leaving behind the poverty to reenter the world she took for granted. A world filled with everything she needed. The children made do with broken-down toys, rusted swing sets, and stew for dinner, yet they laughed and enjoyed life more than many wealthy American children.

"Promise me you will not go back, Emily. It isn't safe for you to be there. Some people do not like the mission and would like to see it gone." His hands gripped the wheel, knuckles white, his voice stern. "Promise."

"You could take me with you when you go," she murmured, knowing he'd refuse.

"It is too dangerous. Do not go there."

But something about the mission drew her. She could help out, she knew she could. Oh, she didn't have huge sums of money to help, but she could hold the babies, tell stories to the older ones, that kind of thing. And she wanted to. She couldn't resist that warm, generous friendship they offered. For the first time since Gran had died, she no longer felt alone. The children had made her part of the group.

Perhaps that's why God had guided her to Rome, to do whatever she could for these little ones.

But what could she do? Emily mused on that all the way home. Then the answer burst upon her brain.

Cece — she might help.

Chapter 5

"You are off to the mission again?" Cece watched as Emily filled her water bottle. "It takes a lot of your time."

"I know. And I feel dreadful leaving you once more." Impossible to believe she'd been here over a month. Cece was now as much a part of her life as Gran had been, listening, probing, and always offering sage advice.

"You know, I've changed my mind. I think I'll stay in this afternoon." She twisted the cap off the bottle, tipped it so the water ran out, feeling guilty that she'd even considered going.

"No, Emily. That would be foolish indeed, for I intend to relax for several hours. *Siesta* is my custom, you understand. I can't imagine running around as you do, in the midday heat." She wagged a hand to cool her red cheeks.

"But I thought the siesta time was mostly in summer." Cece looked flushed, but these lovely Italian spring days certainly were not overly hot.

"Ah. You have caught me in my fable," Cece smiled. "Now I will tell you the truth. It is not so much the heat that bothers me, dear Emmy. It is simply that I am old and weary and must rest to recover my strength." She shrugged in the familiar Latin gesture so common here.

"I'm afraid having me here has been too much for you," Emily murmured, wondering if she should have her ticket changed and go home. But home to what? She still had no idea what came next. But here, in Rome, she could at least help out at the mission.

"It has been my delight and pleasure to have you here. And I think you have benefited also. The young man, you don't think of him with sadness any longer, eh?"

Emily blinked as she realized it was true. She hadn't thought of Tad in days, hadn't wondered if he'd found someone else, hadn't stuffed down the twinge of hurt that he'd left her alone.

"*Si*. I did not think so. Rome has been good for you." Cece's wise blue eyes shone with compassion. "Somehow my beautiful city puts things into perspective, yes?"

"It's true," Emily agreed, musing on the past days spent in the eternal city. "When I walk among the monuments or look at the sculptures, I feel a sense of timelessness, as if I'm but one of many who's trod these stone paths wondering about the future. My petty problems, what do they matter in the course of history?"

"In history, I know not. But to God they matter very much. He cares for you, Emily. He wants your life to be filled with purpose and meaning. He always has a plan." Cece hugged her, then brushed her arthritic hand over Emily's head. "You just have to discover what it is. Perhaps the mission will help you to know what that may be."

"It already has." She tried to put into words what she'd only begun to understand. "True happiness doesn't come from what is around you. Those children — they have nothing. But they are truly happy. They know how to find joy in life, and it bubbles out of them onto me. I thought Tad would make me happy, but he couldn't. Tad wasn't in charge of my happiness."

What was the passage she'd read this morning — the Apostle Paul's words, weren't they? *I've learned whatever state I'm in, to be content.* She'd found contentment in working with the children. If only Nick could understand that.

"I don't like going behind his back," she murmured, as Cece walked her to the front door, where the car she'd hired waited. "And I don't like coercing you, either."

"*Pfui!* I have a friend who has a grandson who likes to drive. It is no hardship for him to take you to the mission when Martino cannot. And I know that you are safe. Nicolo is being unreasonable."

"Maybe." Emily leaned down to brush her lips over the parchment cheek. "Please rest well, Cece. I don't want to wear out my welcome."

"This is not possible. Your welcome is permanent." Cece stood leaning against one of the portico columns, waving as Emily rode away.

There was a mound of things to be done at the mission. Three of the children were ill with a virus that demanded cool pads on their foreheads and plenty of stories to keep their attention until sleep claimed them. Emily was glad to take over, freeing one of the sisters to help with the other children.

Once all three were asleep, she went downstairs to find others working on a craft. Soon there were many little boats made out of sponges, floating in a tub of water outside. Pestered to tell a story about water, Emily spoke of the disciples' fishing escapades. She was lifting the boats out of the water while the children did their homework when Nicolo found her.

"Emily, I asked you not to come here. It is not a safe place for someone like you to be." He looked angry as he glanced around, his eyes resting on the pictures Mario and some other boys had chalked onto the sidewalk. They claimed it was she, and with the bright yellow hair, it was hard to deny it. "You've been here before."

"Yes, and it was perfectly safe. I got a ride here, and the sisters phoned for a taxi to take me back. I was in no danger, Nick."

His lips pinched tight.

"Please try to understand. I enjoy it here so much." She stood her ground, staring up at him, willing him to hear what she needed to say. "I've been all alone since Gran's death. Being around these children is like food for a starving man. I can't *not* come here. Surely you of all people can understand that."

He studied her for a long time. Finally his chest heaved with a sigh and he gave just the slightest nod.

"Promise me you will take extra care. There are always thugs lurking in the side

202

streets in this area. I do not want you to be hurt."

"I won't be." She couldn't contain her grin. "Thank you, Nick. Do you want to see what I brought?" Without waiting for an answer, she grabbed his arm and led him inside, where she'd stashed a small box. "Look."

She held up three of the puppets that she'd bought at the market.

"Aren't they cute? Tonight we are going to have a puppet show. Want to help?"

At first it seemed as though he'd refuse. But finally he nodded.

"What story are we to perform?" he asked, his smile widening when she produced a huge whale. "Ah, Jonah."

Emily didn't understand the odd look that passed over his face as she explained her plan for the story. Nor could she decipher the peculiar glint that sparkled in his dark eyes. She certainly couldn't decode the meaning of his murmured words. "You're an unusual woman, Emily Cain."

But she accepted that he approved of her efforts, and that sent an arrow of warmth straight to her heart. Which was silly. Why did it matter whether Nick approved or not?

"Do you know what I learned today?"

she asked, waiting for his dark head to shake. "Mario told me the legend of Romulus and Remus. How could I have heard so much about Rome and missed that?"

"The Capitoline's she-wolf is an unusual symbol for a city to have." Nick smiled at her nod. "But I'm not sure Mario's version is accurate. Legend has it that Romulus and Remus, the sons of Mars, were tossed into a river by their jealous uncle. The she-wolf dragged them to safety and nursed them. According to the story, Romulus founded Rome on the twenty-first of April in 753 B.C."

"Oh." Emily frowned. "Mario's version was — different."

"I can imagine. He's a born actor." Nick's lips pulled into a crooked smile. "He's certainly taken a liking to you." He brushed his fingertip over her nose. "You've been touched by the sun again. Where were you today?"

"Piazza Navona," she told him, unable to suppress her grin. "I think I'm becoming Italian. I'm starting to use the piazzas as Italians do, like a big living room. I read a book, fed the pigeons, and had my picture done."

"Ah, a portrait. May I see it?"

"Sure." She lifted the page from her bag and held it out. "He was a caricaturist, so it's not exactly me."

Nick studied the drawing for several long moments, then lifted his gaze to her face.

"He was a clever artist, this man. He expressed exactly those things that make you who you are."

Emily stared, surprised by the softness of his voice. "Wh–what do you mean?" she murmured.

"The eyes. It's all there in the eyes. Compassion. Loneliness. Gentleness." Suddenly he blinked, shifted, as if he realized he'd shown her a side of himself she hadn't known existed. "It's a very good picture, Emily." He handed it back.

"Thank you." She tucked it back in her bag, then requested his help to build a temporary stage for the puppets, all the while fully conscious of the stare that remained focused on her when he thought she didn't see. That evening, for the first time since she'd met him, Nick seemed to lose the air of reserve he'd clung to and joined wholeheartedly into the puppet show.

"You are very good with children," she murmured later, as he drove her home. "They seem very comfortable with you.

How long have you been going there?"

"Three years."

Three years — just after his fiancée had died, she guessed.

"Did it help?" she murmured, then wondered if she should have asked.

Nick took his time before responding.

"Not at first. But gradually, bit by bit, I found myself thankful that I was alive, able to enjoy them. The wonderful thing about children is they accept you however you arrive, no questions asked."

"Mmm." The quiet that fell between them was not uncomfortable, but rather that of two companions who'd shared something enjoyable. Emily relaxed fully, her eyes on their surroundings. "This isn't the way back," she murmured.

"No, I thought we'd stop by the Trevi. There's nothing more wonderful than Rome at night. And *la fontana* is very beautiful. Did you throw your coin in already?"

"Oh, yes. More than one." Emily caught her breath as they neared the Colosseum, floodlit from below to emphasize its many arches. "Fantastic, even if it did give me the willies at first."

"More fantastic is the Villa d'Este. The hundred fountains are beautiful at night, even more so than during the day."

"I haven't been," she murmured, wishing she had months — no, years — to see everything Rome — no, Italy — offered.

Nick found a parking space along the crowded streets. Soon they were ambling down the Via delle Muratte to stand at the edge of the most sumptuous fountain in Rome. Water gushed from every part of the statues and from the bas-reliefs perched on heaps of rocks.

"Trevi was once celebrated for its excellent water." Nick's hand lay warm against her elbow, his words soft among those of the many tourists who stood staring. "Would you like to hear the story?"

"Oh, yes. Please." Would she ever tire of listening to Nick's voice?

"Agrippa brought the water to Rome by means of an aqueduct. It is said that the soldiers of Agrippa, looking for water in the Via Collatina in the country, met a maiden who showed them the source of this pure water. Look there, to the right, that is what is depicted. The bas-relief on the left shows Agrippa explaining to Augustus the plan to bring this water to Rome. All of this was built in 1762."

"So long ago, and yet how well it stands the test of time, still spouting its waters." She tugged a coin from her bag and lifted her arm to throw it.

"Oh, no, not like that. And not just one coin." Nick's fingers wrapped around hers. "The first coin is a gift. The second is to assure your return to Rome, but you must turn around and throw it over your shoulder. A silly superstition, some say. But it has become a tradition with tourists." His white teeth gleamed in the darkness. "We must keep up with tradition. Yes?"

Return to Rome. The thought whispered through her like silk. How lovely to come back, again and again, to spend time with Nick the way he'd been tonight, lighthearted, teasing. Most of all, she delighted in the way he could surprise her — like bringing her here to see the fountain at night. He must have seen it a hundred times before, yet for her he made the experience seem new and exciting.

"Oh, yes. By all means, we must uphold tradition. You know what they say, *when in Rome* —"

"*Do as the Romans*," he finished. "Never more apropos than now."

For one long moment, Emily couldn't tear her gaze away from him. Her breath caught, and to regain her calm, she turned her back to the fountain, closed her eyes, and tossed the coin over one shoulder, praying that God would allow her to come back here one day — soon.

"You must see more of Rome by moonlight, but next time we will go to the Piazza Navona to see the fountain of the four rivers. You will think you are having a dream of Aesop's fables."

He was going to take her? Emily couldn't stop the shiver of anticipation that rippled up the arm he held.

"You are chilly. Come, let us go." His fingers threaded through hers automatically as they ambled down the street. She wanted to make the moments last as he spoke of his city's history and she dreamed of being a part of this world.

Back in the car, Nick flicked the heat on low, then took a strange path through a plethora of back roads that seemed almost sinister in their darkness. But before she knew it, they were rolling up the drive in front of Cece's.

"I'm sorry." She reached for the door handle. "I must have fallen asleep." Embarrassment sent a hot flush to her cheeks at Nick's curious smile.

"Yes, you did. But don't worry, you are as beautiful asleep as awake."

"Thank you," she murmured, wondering

how to take the compliment.

He seemed about to say more when the door burst open. Maria stood there wringing her hands, her words spilling over themselves in her haste.

Cece had been taken to the hospital.

Chapter 6

Three days later Emily sat at Cece's bedside, realizing, as she held the frail, parchment-lined hand, how precious this woman had become to her.

"You look so serious, *Carissima.* What troubles you?"

"Nothing." She dredged up a smile, smoothing the blankets with her free hand, but she could tell from Cece's expression that the questions would persist. "I was just thinking what a wonderful time I've had, thanks to Nick and you. I can never thank you enough for inviting me to Rome."

"That sounds as though you are leaving us. Surely your time here is not yet finished?" A troubled frown marred the older woman's face, her lips drew down. "I thought you were intending to stay longer. At least two weeks more, you said yesterday. I had so hoped —"

She closed her eyes, leaning her head back. A tear squeezed out to dance at the end of her lashes, then tumbled down her paper-white cheek.

"Oh, Cece. What's wrong? Are you in pain?" Emily whispered, her heart aching at the older woman's distress. "Please tell me. Perhaps I can help."

"I wish — I wish you would never leave us, Emmy."

The forceful whisper shocked her. Not leave Rome? Emily could only imagine it. To live here always, to revisit history whenever she wanted — such a thing was far beyond anything she'd even dared to dream. But what would she do, how would she live? She was still in the dark about God's reason for bringing her to Rome. How could she possibly stay, especially now, with Cece like this?

"It's kind of you to say that, but I think my being here is the reason you've ended up in this hospital." She caught Cece's sidelong glance at the water jug. "You've overdone when you should have been resting, because of me," she murmured, pouring a glass of water. Tenderly she lifted the thin frail shoulders so her friend could sip. "It's my fault you're ill."

"No! This is not true." Cece lay back against her pillows, her breath short and shallow. "Because of you, Nicolo laughs again. He has lost that dull bored look and begun to take new interest in life, has he not?"

"Well —" Remembering their puppet show, Emily couldn't suppress her grin. "He does love the mission."

"Exactly. But never before would he share it with me. Since Alexandra died and he began to go there, he has not asked, even once, for toys for the little ones. Yet after one puppet show with you, he scours the villa, chuckling like a boy who's found pirate's treasure when he unearths his old playthings. That is because of you, Emmy. You have brought joy to Nico."

"I only suggested there might be some old toys lying around." And spent hours stitching tattered rabbit ears and securing floppy tails while she waited to know how Cece would fare. "I was glad to help. It felt good to be needed."

"Yes, but you also feel a deep compassion for this mission, no?"

"Yes. What I do is so little, but they act as if I'm really contributing. Being there — it fills my heart," she explained simply.

"Do you think God might be telling you something, my dear Emmy?" Cecelia's sharp eyes probed as deeply as her words. "You care for Nico, don't you? The old love has passed away, the pain has disappeared. And in its place sprouts a fresh, new joy. Not only for the children, I think." She winked.

Emily laughed, then grew sober, thinking. She liked Nick, but — more?

"At first I found him standoffish. I knew what you and Gran had planned. He knew, too. It made things awkward between us. But now . . ." She closed her eyes. "I don't know, Cece. I've been so confused about the next step, about where God is directing me. I prayed over and over to be shown what God would have me do, but going back to college somehow doesn't feel right. I'm tired of studying moldy books. I want to *do* something."

"And you shall have your chance." Nico walked through the door, kissed his grandmother's cheek, then grinned at Emily, looking every bit the carefree man his grandmother had suggested he'd become. "Sister Claudia telephoned me this afternoon. Children keep showing up at the mission, asking about your next puppet show. Apparently you've become famous."

"They liked it that much?" Sheer delight sent her spirits soaring. "I'm so glad. I've been working on a new show, you know. It's about the battle of Jericho. I even made

214

some tiny trumpets for the puppets."

"This is another reason why you cannot go yet, Emmy. What about the children? They've come to expect your shows." Cece turned to her grandson. "Tell her, Nico. Tell her she cannot go yet. Tell her that she is not to blame for my silly illness or for my presence in the hospital."

"Is that what you think, Emily?" Nick's dark gaze brimmed with compassion. "That is foolish. Nonna had her heart disease long before you arrived. You must not blame yourself. She loves having you here, even though we've not fallen in with our grandmothers' plans." He winked at Cece. "You thought I didn't know what you were up to? But, of course, I couldn't *not* know. You are too obvious, *Bellissima*."

He flicked a gentle finger against her pale, thin cheek, his voice tender but firm.

"Emily and I are adults, Nonna; we make our own decisions. I understand her need to return to her home and so must you. She is no doubt lonely for her friends. A few more days, then her holiday is over and her life goes on."

Emily couldn't have uttered a word, even if her throat hadn't been choked. Lonely? Since Gran's death, she'd never been less lonely than she was right here. But it was obvious that Nick thought of her as nothing more than a guest, a tourist to chauffeur around when the mood struck. That hurt. Why?

Because she loved him.

The truth hit her hard and she blinked, hoping no one had noticed. Nick's attention remained on his grandmother, but Cece's gaze was on her, soft, compassionate. She gave a slight nod.

"Off you go, Nico. Offer your daily ranting about my welfare to the doctors, or they will think you are ill. When you finish, you shall take Emily to present her puppets." She shooed him from the room, waited until the door closed, then held out her arms. "Oh, *poverina*. I am so sorry. My so smart grandson is as blind as a bat where you're concerned."

"It's all right." Nonetheless, Emily sank into the embrace, relishing the gentle touch and soft words. "I–I didn't realize, you see. We'd become friends. I don't know when —"

"The heart doesn't always follow orders from the head. And my Nico is a most charming man, when he isn't brooding. Don't you think so?" She winked, then chuckled at Emily's blush.

"Most charming. But what I think

doesn't matter, Cece. Nick sees me as nothing more than a guest, a tourist who visits for a short time. He doesn't care for me — that way." She drew away, dabbed at her eyes, anxious that Nick notice nothing when he returned.

Cece remained silent for a few minutes, her bright eyes only hinting at the thoughts inside her silver head. Finally she patted the side of her bed.

"Tell me, Emily, have you been to the Pantheon?" She frowned, then nodded. "Yes, I remember you said you'd visited. When you were there, did they tell you that the Pantheon is the most perfect of buildings? The height and diameter of the interior are equal, you see. This is unusual."

"Yes, and light and air enter through an opening in the center of the dome." Emily bit her lip to stem her impatience. "What are you trying to tell me, Cece?" What had the Pantheon to do with Nick?

"The workmanship is superb. Did you know that the best time to view the interior is not while the sun shines, but during a thunderstorm when lightning flashes, illuminating the shadows and the treasures they hide?" She waited a moment, then smiled. "But for that hole in the ceiling, we might never see them."

There was meaning to her words. Emily just had to figure out what that meaning was. Right now, illumination eluded her. Finally Cece spoke, her voice quiet.

"Nicolo has only recently let the light back into his life. Give him time to let it seek out the shadows and illuminate his fears. I think you will find your patience rewarded." Her bright eyes flickered, certainty in their depths. "God did not bring you here to us without a reason. We have only to wait and see what that reason might be. Search your heart, Emily. Ask Him."

"Are you ready to leave, Emily?" Nick glanced from one to the other warily. "What are you two talking about?"

"The Pantheon. Your grandmother was explaining the dome."

"Was she?" He walked across the room, kissed Cece's cheek, then straightened. His voice softened, gentled. "Remind me to question what she told you. History is not her forte. In fact, she always gets the dates wrong."

"Oh, she wasn't talking about dates. And I'm quite sure that, in this particular case, she is exactly right. At least, I hope so." Emily gathered up her bag, kissed Cece good night, then followed him out of the room.

But at the door she paused, glancing over one shoulder. Was Cece right? Did God have something special in store, something Emily hadn't imagined when she'd left Chicago? Something that would fill her future with hope and promise?

These thoughts and a thousand others occupied her mind until Nick stopped the car in front of Cece's gorgeous home.

"I have to get something upstairs and make a phone call," he told her. "I'll only be a few moments."

Left alone, Emily abandoned the car to wander in Cece's garden. She sank onto the smooth hardness of a garden bench, her attention drawn by the riot of colors and blooms that spilled out of containers, climbed up the walls and crept across the flagstones, each petal, each stem individually created for a specific reason by the Creator.

Consider the lilies of the field. They neither sow nor reap. Yet Solomon, in all his glory, was not arrayed like one of these.

She closed her eyes. *God, I'm so confused. I believe you sent me to Rome for some reason I don't yet understand. I love the children, I want to help them, yet I have no money to give and I must soon leave this place. But, Lord, my heart longs to stay here, with Nick. I don't understand these feelings. Are they just me, or did You plan it all along? Please show me Your way. In Jesus' name. Amen.*

The thump of Nick's footsteps down the stairs echoed through the house, and Emily knew it was time to go. Her decision was made. While at the mission, she would relish every moment with the children, for that was a gift too precious to waste. And tomorrow she'd work hard to understand Nick's obsession with the past.

But just for tonight, while the big round moon cast its orange glow over the many domes and arches of this spectacular city, she'd stop worrying about tomorrow and concentrate on savoring whatever precious moments she was given to share with Nick. She'd memorize his laugh, imprint the sparkle in his dancing eyes as he teased the children with the puppets. She'd tuck each memory deep inside her heart.

And she'd leave the rest up to God.

Chapter 7

A week later, Nick leaned one shoulder against the stone wall and watched Emily mesmerize the children who'd gathered for yet another of her puppet shows. She was an expert at drawing out the suspense in her stories so that no one, not even Mario, dared twitch a muscle until she announced, "The end."

Somehow, in ways Nick had only begun to fathom, she managed to touch each of the children, not just with her funny stories, but also with her abundant hugs, the featherlight brush of her dainty hand, and the comfort of her sweet words. It was with her that they shared their deepest secrets, and to whom they came with their needs.

Just this evening he'd watched her slip a sandwich to a boy in the audience whom he knew had not eaten dinner. For another she'd torn up a skirt so that together they could sew the girl's mother a shawl as a birthday gift. They loved her, all of them, and he freely admitted that he was jealous of the attention that she showered upon them.

But he was also worried. What would happen when she left, what would the children do? He'd tried to envision it, but the picture wouldn't appear. Emily was as much a part of the mission as Sister Claudia. In fact, he'd grown used to her presence in his life — teasing her over the breakfast table, watching her care for Cece, listening as she told Maria where she'd been, what she'd seen.

But the highlight of Nick's day always came when her green eyes grew huge and shone with delight when she gazed at the old Roman ruins he loved. He'd drawn upon every history manual he could find, scoured out the most oblique of facts, toured the city to find the best places to show her at night, after they left the mission.

They shared that, at least. Emily might be from a land far away, she might be used to new homes with all the latest gadgets and men familiar with her way of life, but none of it seemed to matter when it came to his city. She savored the past, drew parallels from it to her present life.

What would he do when she left?

The stark bleakness of that question

made him push away from the wall and wander outside, to the children's playground. He sat on a rusted swing and stared upward, fixed his eyes on the stars, and remembered Cece's words.

"Emily isn't here by chance, Nico. God sent her to be used when that mission most needed her. I also think He sent her for you. If you'd only open your eyes and your heart, you'd see I'm right."

But much as he loved Nonna, she wasn't right. He'd known that for three years. He'd promised Alexandra that there would never be anyone else, that she alone would hold his heart forever. So many plans they'd made — three children, dark-eyed, button-nose brunets like their mother. Alexandra would continue with her fashion designing, of course. But she'd find a nanny, someone who would ensure their children had the best of everything.

Like a faithless thief, the thought crept into his brain. Would Emily leave her children to a nanny? He shoved the question away, angry at the disloyalty of it. Emily didn't have a career; she had no plans for the future. She didn't even know what she would do tomorrow. Alexandra and he had made plans for the next fifty years. To turn his back on that would be to betray the love he'd felt for her.

"Alexandra is dead, Nico. She wouldn't expect you to pay homage for the rest of your life."

But Nonna was wrong. He owed Alexandra his loyalty, but Cece wouldn't understand that. She didn't know the questions he'd begun to ask himself in the days before Alexandra's death. She'd wanted them to move to Milan, not right away, but eventually. It made sense, her career would push forward there. But his life was here. Nonna was here. Home was Roma.

But he hadn't told her that. Instead, he'd let Alexandra think he was willing to leave his life behind and begin again, for her. The more she talked about the future, the more he'd begun to wonder if he'd made a mistake. The night she'd died, he'd asked her to put their marriage plans on hold, told her that he was no longer certain of their future together. The love he'd once been so sure of was shaken by a little thing like location. How could it have withstood the test of time, children, diverging careers?

"Is anything wrong, Nick?" Emily stood beside him, her slight figure barely discernable in the poor light.

"Just thinking." If he turned his head just a bit, the spicy scent of the Persian rose fragrance he'd helped her choose in the market last week assaulted his senses. It was like her — soft, unexpected, yet quietly appealing.

"It must be a rather unpleasant thought."

A hint of laughter resonated through her voice. He twisted to look at her face, saw her smile.

"You were frowning quite fiercely," she murmured. His silence made her frown. "Is something wrong, Nick?"

"Not wrong exactly. I was just thinking about when you leave Rome."

"A week. That's all I have left." The smile was gone from her voice, her eyes no longer danced. In fact, her entire body seemed to droop. "I was just waiting for Cece. I didn't want to leave before I knew she was feeling better."

"I'm glad you stayed." That was the truth. He enjoyed knowing his grandmother had someone watching to be sure she didn't overdo, someone who would ensure she rested at the appropriate times. Someone who could handle the everyday directions for the staff.

And he enjoyed coming home to find

Emily waiting for him. They often shared a cool drink on the patio before Maria announced dinner, which had been bumped up a little earlier so Cece could join them, and so that they would have plenty of time to spend at the mission.

"Actually I was thinking of how much the children would miss you. You've grown so close to them. It will be a terrible wrench for them. Have you told them yet?" He glanced up in time to see her blond head shake. Tears welled in her eyes.

"I've been so selfish," she exclaimed. "I haven't been thinking of them at all, but of me, of how much I'm going to miss not being here for Emilio's first birthday or to watch Sophia say her first word. But they will have it much harder, won't they, Nick?"

He felt ashamed by his own words when her head bowed and he heard the words slip from her lips.

"Perhaps it would have been better if I had never come here," she whispered.

"Of course it wouldn't have been better." He bristled with anger at his own carelessness. Why was it that whenever he spoke to Emily, he couldn't find the right words? Time after time he'd blurted out something which she'd taken the wrong way, and he hadn't bothered to correct her impression. Well, not this time!

"They've loved having you here, Emily. You've done so much for them, given them love and understanding that money could never buy. And you've taught them what it means to be a follower of Jesus. That's worth a great deal." He saw her eyebrows rise and stopped. "I just meant that perhaps we should prepare them, ease the shock a bit," he muttered, wishing he'd minded his own business.

"Actually, I'd planned to tell them the ascension story one of these nights. Perhaps I could tie that in to my leaving." Her furrowed brow told him how hard she was thinking. "You know the kind of thing — people leave, but if we all love God and obey Him, we see each other in heaven again." She lifted her head, stared at him. "Would that be all right?"

A wave of tenderness washed over him as he stared into her eyes. She was so concerned for the children, and so careless about her own needs. But leaving Rome would mean she would go back to — what? Cece had insisted Emily had no family in America. What kind of a life would she make there?

"Nick?"

He blinked, saw the question in her eyes.

"Would you pray with me? I need God's help to do this. I love these kids very much. It will be hard to say good-bye when the time comes."

"Of course I'll pray with you." He accepted her outstretched hand, watched her gulp, and wondered if he was doing the right thing by letting her go. Did she know how much he and his grandmother would miss her bubbly presence in their dull lives? How much he'd miss the sparkle she brought to each day?

"Dear Jesus, the children in this mission are special to You. You know the exact number of hairs on their heads and what they long for most in their hearts. I don't want to hurt them, Father. Let me be a lamp and light for You. Amen." She sighed, then glanced up at him. "I'll start preparing tomorrow night."

"I didn't mean to hurt you, Emily," he murmured, fingers still entwined with hers. "I know you love them. I just thought —"

"I know. And you're right. I can't leave it till the last minute. But it hurts to think of leaving." She choked back a sob, tugged her hand from his. "I need some cheering up, Nick. Can we go somewhere bright and happy and fun tonight? I don't want to look at anything from the past, and I don't want to think about the future. I just want to be around people who are laughing and singing. Is that okay?"

He nodded, forcing a smile.

"Of course. We'll have coffee and dessert in one of the sidewalk cafés and watch the world go by."

Later, as they wandered down the Via Veneto, Nick kept her hand tucked into his arm, pausing when she did to look at the wares of the street peddlers. He encouraged her to have a new portrait sketched by a diffcrent artist and laughed with her when the balloon she'd been given blew up and away into the night sky.

At her request, Nick drove to the Piazza Navona and stood beside her while she stared into the aquamarine water that spurted out of the fountain of the four rivers. Emily shivered once, and he moved to wrap his arm around her shoulder, cuddling her against his side as they stared at the four figures. He could have told her that the work of Bernini was meant to represent the Danube, the Ganges, the Nile, and the Rio de la Plata. He could have explained that the piazza now occupied the former stadium of Domitian, that it could once hold up to thirty thousand spectators. He could have given her the age of the statue and the piazza and pointed out several artifacts nearby.

He could have, but he didn't.

Suddenly none of that seemed important. The only thing he could think about, the one fact that imprinted his brain, was that in seven days she wouldn't be there to share it with him and he would be lonelier than he'd ever been in his life.

"Emily," he whispered, wanting to tell her something, anything, that would ease the pain he saw on her beautiful face.

She turned to him, her green eyes wide, questioning, molten hair blowing in the breeze. Suddenly Nick knew that whatever he'd hoped to convey couldn't be compressed into mere words. There was only one way he could explain, and he hoped she would understand.

His gaze honed in on her lovely mouth, and he bent his head and touched his lips to hers, praying she'd understand, delighted that his prayer had been answered when her arm reached around his waist and her lips returned his caress.

He eased back, stared into her upturned face as his emotions swirled around him. She was young, beautiful, and she had her whole life before her, a chance to do anything she wished. And he wanted to spend the rest of his life with her.

The shock of that held him immobile.

Then a cool breeze whipped the fountain water in a spray that spattered over them like a hard dash of reality. Emily stared at him, and he watched as the resignation crashed over her like a wave she couldn't avoid. With a sob, she pulled away, turned her back on him.

It was a good thing she did, for Nick knew what had to happen. No matter how deeply Emily was buried in his heart, he couldn't ask her to stay. God's plan for him didn't include that.

"Let's go home, Nick," she whispered when a group of merrymakers invaded their privacy moments later. "Please take me home."

"Yes." But as he drove back to Cece's, escorted Emily from the car and into the villa, he begged God to take away the feelings, to send him back to the self-imposed hermit he'd become before she'd pulled him back into life.

Later, as he sat in his grandmother's garden and watched the sun rise, Nick realized how foolish his prayer had been.

Nothing would ever make him forget Emily.

It was childish to pretend otherwise.

Chapter 8

It was her last full day in Rome.

Ever since she'd risen this morning, each action felt as if it occurred in slow motion. That feeling persisted as Emily filled her water bottle and stowed it in her bag, made sure her map was tucked inside, along with a tissue and an apple. Maybe if she could prolong the day, draw it out to the very last second, she wouldn't have to leave.

"Are you ready, my dear?"

Emily turned to smile at the precious woman she'd grown to love.

"More than ready, Cece. I deliberately left the catacombs till last, but now I wish I'd opted to go earlier. I could have spent today in St. Peter's."

Cece wrapped an arm around her waist and walked with her to the door.

"Because you could have prayed there?" she asked, one eyebrow quirked. She read Emily's eyes and shook her head. "Dear one, you must remember that God hears His beloved children no matter where they are. The catacombs are as good a place to speak to Him as any and perhaps better than most. They will help remind you that our God is not dead, that the same One who cared for those poor souls is still working today. Think on His goodness, Emmy. You will find the solace you seek."

"I love you." She hugged the tiny frame close, breathed in the sweet lilac scent that would always be Cece.

"I love you, too. Now off you go and enjoy your day." If Cece's smile looked a little forced, she wasn't allowing Emily to see it.

"You're sure you'll be all right?" Emily couldn't help asking. "You wouldn't rather I stay here, keep you company?"

"Watch me while I sleep?" Cece shook her white head firmly. "No. I'm perfectly well, Emmy. You go and enjoy your day. Just be sure to return in time for dinner. Maria has something special planned." Cece kissed her cheek. "There you are, your taxi awaits."

Emily's emotions churned wildly as they drove through the familiar streets. One last day. That's all there was left. Very well then. Hadn't she given her future to God? Now she had to trust that He would not let her stumble or fall.

This morning she would revisit St. Peter's and allow herself one last look. By the time the sun was hot and the day warm, it would feel good to wander through the catacombs. Secretly she'd hoped to see Nick leading a class through the famous basilica, but there was no sight of him in St. Peter's Square, nor did she happen to meet him while pondering the Sistine Chapel ceiling. Perhaps that was just as well, for as she stared up at Michelangelo's magnificent frescoes, she was reminded of God's unwavering love for His children. A sense of peace washed into her soul.

After enjoying a slice of piping hot pizza on the Spanish steps, she sipped her water and watched the couples who filled the piazza. They looked so happy, and for a moment, the impact of leaving grabbed at her. But Emily fought back, whispering a prayer for help. By the time she'd stored her bottle in her bag and strolled to the catacombs of St. Sebastian, she was reconciled to following the path on which God led her.

The solemnity of the catacombs felt sadly eerie. She stood to one side, watching as members of the Franciscan order moved through the underground cemetery in respectful silence.

"A magnificent basilica over this spot was built in the fourth century to honor the apostles Peter and Paul. It later received the precious relic of Peter."

Delighted and surprised by the familiar sound of that whispered voice, Emily whirled to face Nick.

"I didn't know you were coming here," she murmured, mindful of the silence surrounding them.

"I had a few hours off and thought you might like company." He led her down a pathway that wound through the burial grounds. "Excavations began in 1915, but still they continue today. A particularly important series of buildings have been found, which were dedicated to the two apostles at a time when it was illegal to bury the dead inside Rome."

For the first time, Emily heard little of the actual content of Nick's words. Instead she reveled in the pleasure of listening to the timbre of his low voice, of the brush of his arm against her, the gentle way he guided her through the barrel-vaulted complexes. When he finally led her out, Emily knew she couldn't walk away without at least trying — one last time.

"It's early yet. I know Maria is making a special dinner before we go to the mission, but I wonder if you'd like to see one last thing." Nick's voice was quiet, but brimming with determination, as if he had something he intended to say and would not be put off.

"I'd love to see whatever you'd like to show me," she murmured, trying to quell the tiny flicker of hope that would not be dashed. "Is it far?"

"No." He walked her back to his car, helped her inside, then headed away from the city, climbing steadily to the top of a hill. "It's not much really. Just the *campagna,* the countryside." He waited for her to join him on the crest, then waved a hand to indicate the vista in front of them.

"Not everyone appreciates or understands the Roman countryside," he murmured in hushed tones as the sun blazed its last few red rays over them, then began a slow and steady descent beneath the horizon.

Emily watched, holding her breath until the last faint flicker cast a shadowed light across the ruins in front of them.

"At one time this land was full of patrician tombs, military roads, and of villas where noble families lived. There were great aqueducts just over there that brought abundant supplies of water to the baths and the fountains, and irrigated the gardens and vineyards. The rest of the world benefited greatly from Rome's influence, which was once contained within these seven hills."

"It's a wonderful heritage and a magnificent country," she whispered, unsure of the meaning behind this strange litany. "You have every right to be proud of your city."

"I love Roma." He smiled that lopsided grin that didn't quite reach his eyes. "But that is not why I brought you here."

"Oh."

"No. I had another reason." He turned, pointed to a small cross that stood opposite them, on the other side of the road. "Alexandra died here."

That caught her by surprise.

"I–I'm so sorry, Nick. You must have loved her very much." Why did it hurt so much to think of Nick loving someone else?

"I thought I did. Later, well, I had questions. We had — different views of life. I'm not at all sure a marriage between us would have worked."

"All couples have problems." She didn't quite know what to say, so Emily whispered a prayer for help. "But once you've made the commitment, you work things out. I'm sure the two of you would have learned to compromise."

"Probably."

But he didn't sound certain. Instead he turned his back on that side of the road, stared down at the magnificence that had stood before them and had disappeared with the erosion of time. One hand raked through his hair.

"I came here many times after she died. I didn't know what else to do, and I felt that here, alone, I could talk to God." Suddenly he faced her, his palms cupped her face. "I made God a promise here, Emily."

"Oh." The hairs on her arm prickled, but it wasn't from the breeze. A terrible feeling assailed her, and she clung to the faith she'd found earlier.

"After her death, I realized that God's plan for me did not include marriage. He led me to the mission, and I've found joy there, and happiness."

"Is it enough?" she whispered, wondering if she dared to tell him her feelings. "Will watching those kids grow up replace seeing your own?"

"It has to." His thumbs brushed against her cheeks, his eyes dark and sad. "Don't you understand? I made a promise to God that I would be content to help at the mission, to do what I could there. His plan for me doesn't include anything more, no matter how much I want it."

"How do you know that?" she demanded, jerking out of his grasp, as the tears welled in her eyes. "How can you be so sure?"

"I just am. Please understand. You are a wonderful woman, Emily. The children adore you because your heart is big and you give constantly. Cece adores you, too."

"And you?" She waited, breath suspended, for an answer she knew he couldn't give her.

"I–I care about you, Emily. Truly." He let out a pent-up breath, his shoulders slumped. "But I have no business doing so. I promised God, and I will not go back on that. Besides, we're worlds apart. I'm years older than you, from a different culture, a different land. I'm a simple teacher, I have nothing to offer you."

He did. If only he loved her, it would be more than she'd dared hope or dream for. But she wasn't going to argue or debate it. If God had chosen Nick for her, He would find a way to work things out. At least she'd learned that much from her days in Rome. Her life was in God's hands. He alone could open doors, or hearts.

As she stared into the night sky and the ruins that lay broken and crushed through the ages, Emily could only rejoice that she'd come to Rome. Tad hadn't been the right man for her, and even though she'd been bitter about his leaving, she realized now that his actions had saved her from making a huge mistake.

"I've upset you. I'm sorry, Emily. You have a right to be angry with me after what we shared."

Though it cost her greatly, Emily reached out, touched his arm with her fingers, feeling the warmth of his skin transmit to hers.

"I'm not angry, Nick. Not at all. You've taught me so much about your country, about the past, and from that, I've learned to look to the future." Emily smiled at the skeptical frown on his face. "It's true. Being here, getting to know you and your grandmother, it's been a chance for me to think beyond my little world and consider life in a broader scope, in terms of eternity."

"You really mean this?" His hand moved to cover hers, eyes quizzical.

She nodded.

"Yes. You know what's in your heart,

Nick, and that's between you and God." She stood on her tiptoes and brushed her lips against his cheek. "I'm glad to have known you, Nicolo Fellini. You're a strong, caring man who has trusted God with his future. That's all any of us can do. I respect your desire to be true to your promise."

Then she turned and walked back to the car, climbed inside, and waited to be driven back to the villa.

I've done my best, Lord. Wherever You lead, I'll follow. The prayer slipped from her lips, as she watched Nick survey the hills once more before turning to walk toward her.

I love him, God. More than I ever dreamed. But I want to do Your will.

Chapter 9

He'd done everything he could think of to steel himself for the evening ahead, but as they walked into the mission later that evening, Nick knew Emily would not be the only one fighting her emotions tonight.

"*Ciao, piccolina,*" she laughed as a tiny girl toddled over to hug her legs. "It was such a hot day, and yet here you are, brimming with energy." She kissed the downy soft cheek, remaining hunkered down to receive the endless round of hugs that the other children offered.

"I love you, too," she whispered in each tiny ear. As usual, their probing fingers found a way to touch her shining mane of golden hair, eyes huge.

Emily laughed at them, her gaze sparkling with love as they poked and prodded her pockets for the treats she always brought. Nick moved back and simply watched as she showered her attention on each child, listening and nodding as they explained their day in minute detail.

"So much love to give," his grandmother

had said after dinner, while Emily prepared for their mission visit.

He could not help but agree.

"You're staring at me," she whispered, as she passed him to mop up the purple juice a chubby hand had spilled. "Do I have something on my face?"

Nick shook his head, but no words would emerge from his choked throat.

"Well, what then? You look very — odd." She glanced down, saw the spot where a bit of melon clung to her sundress and blushed, her cheeks rosy with embarrassment. "I'm such a mess," she giggled, plucking the fruit off. "You must be embarrassed."

He wasn't, not at all. He was proud of her, as if it were somehow his right to crow to anyone that cared to listen that Emily Cain was a woman to be prized.

Indignation surged inside. Why? Why did this have to happen now? He'd grown accustomed to his lonely life, he'd put aside his dreams and hopes and resigned himself to bypass all the things his colleagues and friends were now enjoying.

"Nick?" She stood waiting, her smile fading as she stared into his eyes.

"You look fine," he murmured, reaching to brush a bit of cookie from a strand of her hair. "You look wonderful."

"Don't be sad, Nick," she whispered, her green eyes brimming with tears. "God is good. He knows the desires of my heart. He will bring things to pass in His own time. But I need you to be strong tonight, to help me say good-bye. Please help me."

How could he refuse her?

"Come, children, gather round. Emily has something to say."

"Thank you." Her hand brushed his for only a second before she turned to those clamoring for her attention. "You all know this is my last time with you." She stopped, controlled the tremble in her voice. "Tomorrow I will get on a plane and fly back to my home in America."

Thirty-five sets of button bright eyes stared at her.

"I'm going to miss you so much," she continued. "And I'm going to pray that one day God brings me back here, to see you again. Will you pray for me, too?"

Nick found a path through the dozens of brown arms and legs, then strode across the room until at last he was outside the building, in the little courtyard where the children played. He tilted his head back and filled his lungs with great gulps of air.

"It isn't so easy to deny your feelings, is it, Nico?"

He jerked around, stunned to see his grandmother sitting on a small chair, wrapped in a thick shawl.

"What are you doing here?" he demanded, automatically checking her color. "You are supposed to be at home, resting."

"Am I?" She shrugged. "I did not feel like resting. Tonight I felt like watching my grandson push away the gift God has given him."

"Don't start, Grandmother. You know my feelings." Anger nipped at him, mingling with guilt that he'd spoken so sharply to his beloved Nonna. "Happily ever after is not for everyone. I am prepared to do what I promised. Isn't that enough?"

"It is if God has asked this of you," she murmured, her eyes dark in the shadowy yard. "But has He asked this, my son? Or is this something you've done — locked away your heart so you won't have to suffer as you did when Alexandra died?"

"How can you ask that?" He paced back and forth across the yard, trying to ignore what she'd said, but the words would not be silenced. "You know that His plan is for me to remain alone."

"I think that was your plan, Nico, and

that you've convinced yourself that God had asked it of you."

He couldn't believe Nonna was saying this.

"What is the first thing you learned about God? Was it not that He is love? Emily came here because you wrote her, yes. But it was an idea that began long before your birth and it was supposed to happen when her mother was alive. Don't you see? God chose to send Emily to us at a time when she needed us."

"Sì. This is true." Nick nodded. Yes, he understood that. She'd been hurting and somehow among the ruins she'd found peace and joy.

"Could not that same God, the one you both serve — could He not have drawn the two of you together for His own plan?" She saw his frown and snapped her fingers. "Think of it this way, Nico. Your trust has been in yourself, in your ability to keep a promise you made. That is wrong. We do not trust in ourselves, but in the God who chose us. 'Blessed is the man who trusts in the Lord and has made the Lord his hope and confidence.' Is that what you've done, Nico? Or is your hope and confidence in yourself?"

"Cece! I didn't know you'd be here."

Emily stood in the doorway, glancing back and forth between them. "Have I interrupted something?"

"Of course not. Come. I have brought a huge cake which Maria insists you are to share with the children." She rose and, using her cane, moved slowly across the courtyard. "Come, Nico."

"In a moment," he murmured, watching as Emily threaded her arm through the frail woman's and helped ease her way. "I'll be there in a moment."

Moments later the children's voices echoed outside, but Nick heard little of that. His eyes were fixed on something much farther away.

"But what is the truth, Father?" he whispered. "Please show me the truth. Is Cece right — is it fear that I cling to?"

"I'm sorry you had to get up so early just to drop me at the airport." Emily offered the silly polite words, wishing desperately that she had something wonderful to say, something that would shatter the silence between them and bring back that easy camaraderie of past days.

"It is nothing. I was not asleep."

"No, I guessed not." In truth of fact, Nick looked like he hadn't gone to bed.

Black stubble covered his jutting Roman chin. His eyes were bloodshot, with tiny lines fanning out around them. The only things that looked fresh were his clothes, the perfectly tailored black pants and pristine white shirt that emphasized his Latin heritage.

How would she live without seeing him every day?

Emily thrust the thought from her. Faith didn't mean trusting for a moment, or an hour. Faith meant letting go and waiting for God. However long that took.

"It's very busy this morning, isn't it? I'm afraid you won't find a spot to park."

He grunted noncommittal agreement, slowing the car to a crawl as they approached the departure level. Finally, another vehicle pulled away, and Nick directed his car into its spot.

"You can only stay here for five minutes," she murmured, staring at the sign. This was not how she'd planned to say good-bye, but perhaps a quick break was best.

He shrugged, climbed out of the car, and unlocked the trunk, one eye on the policeman who was now headed their way.

"Listen, Nick. There's no reason you should get a ticket. This suitcase has wheels, and I can find my way to the proper gate." She took her suitcase from him and snapped out the handle. "Let's just say good-bye here."

Using sheer willpower, Emily dragged the smile to her lips, all the while her senses soaked up every memory she would need to sustain her in the weeks ahead.

"Thank you for showing me all the sights and for explaining everything. I couldn't have wished for a better tour guide, even though we got off on the wrong foot at first."

He frowned, opening his mouth to reply, but Emily couldn't wait, couldn't listen to the words. Not now.

"Ciao." The policeman stood on the curb, obviously prepared to ask Nick to move.

Seizing her moment, Emily whispered good-bye.

"Thank you," she murmured. But that didn't say all that was in her heart, so she stood on tiptoes, wrapped her arms around his neck, pressed her lips against his cheek, then blurted out the one thing she'd promised herself she would not say.

"I love you, Nick Fellini. I thank God for sending me here to meet you. I wish you only the best. Good-bye, my love." Then she turned and walked into the airport as quickly as she could, dragging her suitcase behind.

By clenching her jaw and walking straight ahead, she managed to find the appropriate gate. But once there, she could control her emotions no longer. Flopping down in a seat, she hunched over and let the tears flow, wishing they could ease the ache in her soul.

She'd arrived here, bitter and angry about a future she wouldn't share. Now she would leave, realizing that what she'd thought was love for Tad came nowhere near the overwhelming tenderness she felt for Nick.

"Please help me, God," she whispered, oblivious to the sounds around her. "Your will be done."

Chapter 10

Nick stared at the policeman, and wondered what he was saying. Nothing made sense this morning.

Emily loved him?

Into his mind swam the picture of her, green eyes shiny with a lambent glow that radiated from deep inside. And that beautiful hair — coiled about her head like a veil of gold. She loved him. Was such a thing possible? Shouldn't he have known, have seen — something?

But it was there, he realized, thinking back on the times they'd spent together. The day he'd taken her to his special place and tried to explain, hadn't he known it then? Wasn't that why he'd tried so hard to make her understand that a relationship between them was futile — because he knew she was different, that she was someone he couldn't walk away from?

So what was he doing?

Cece thought he'd put the barriers there himself. All night he'd struggled with that — begged and pleaded with God to show him the right way. Now with the clarity of the early morning sun flooding the airport tarmac, he understood that God had never asked such a thing of him. It had been his own guilt, his own fear, his own mistrust of love that had tricked him into believing that he could not love Emily, that to do so was to consign Alexandra to some terrible faint memory.

But he had loved Alexandra. Perhaps they would have married; he didn't know. Only God did. And in His infinite wisdom, God had sent him a young woman who cared about the things that he did, who threw herself into life because she believed God was in charge.

And in a short time she would fly away, believing he hadn't loved her enough.

"Mi scusi," he muttered to the surprised policeman. He should explain, tell him why he was leaving his car behind. But there was no time.

Nick raced into the airport, scanned the monitors, and headed for the gate he knew Emily had taken. He fiddled impatiently while security scanned him, then hurried down the gleaming walk, his eyes searching.

"Emily?"

She glanced up, turquoise eyes damp with tears that lay on her cheeks. Blond bits of hair stuck to her face, but he wiped them away.

"I love you, Emily. Will you marry me, stay in Rome, help with the mission? Until God tells us to do something different?" He caught her hands, drew her upright. "I steeped myself so deeply in history, I almost missed the present. I almost missed loving you."

"Oh, Nick." She stood on her tiptoes, threw her arms around his neck, and returned his kiss with fervor. "I love you, too. I'd love to marry you."

Several moments later he became aware that they were attracting attention.

"Let's go home to Nonna," he whispered.

The boarding announcement cut off her response.

Emily stared into his eyes.

"Do you trust me, Nick? Do you trust God?"

"Yes, of course." He frowned. "Why do you ask?"

"Because before I can marry you, I need to go home. There's something I have to get."

"But — we could go together, after we're married."

She shook her head, her eyes dark. "Can't you trust me, Nick? Can't you trust Him?"

To let her go, so soon after he'd found her — it was asking a lot. But finally he nodded.

"Go home. Settle your affairs. Because when you next return to Rome, I will never let you go." He held her, cherishing the love they shared.

"I won't want to leave," she reassured him, her smile huge. "It won't take me long. Two weeks, no more. I promise."

The final boarding call separated them. He walked her as far as he could and kissed her one last time.

"I love you, Emily."

"I love you, Nick."

Then she disappeared.

Emily slid a hand over the delicate satin folds of her wedding dress, her eyes riveted on the mirror that showed her grandmother's dress in all its beauty.

"It's a most lovely gown, *Carissima*. I'm glad you brought it. Your grandmother is the one who started this." Cece leaned over to kiss her cheek. "Even now I know she is watching from heaven. I can feel her smile inside here." She patted her heart.

"She always told me that one day I would wear her dress."

A soft rap on the bedroom door broke the silence.

"I've waited a long time to get married." Nick's low growl penetrated the thick wooden door, a hint of worry at its edges. "How much longer, Emily?"

With the help of her cane, Cece walked to the door, opened it just enough to slip through, and wrapped her arm in his.

"No longer. We are ready. Let us go to the garden to wait for Emily."

Emily took one last look, then whispered a prayer. Today she knew exactly where she was going. God had led her on a path filled with discovery, but many more awaited her as Nick's wife.

She opened the door, walked across the hall, and began her descent down the stairs. A sheaf of blood-red roses from Nick waited at the bottom. She gathered them into her arms, sniffed their fragrance, then made her way to the garden where he waited.

Nick took his time staring at her, his eyes widening at the beauty of her gown.

"Was it worth the wait?" she whispered, before the minister could begin.

He lifted her hand to his lips and kissed it, grazing the diamond ring he'd given her on her return.

"You, my darling Emily, are always worth waiting for."

Dear Reader,

A Roman holiday is unlike any other. From the first Bernini statue towering in the piazza, to the soft gush of the Trevi fountain, to the inspiration of the Vatican, to the reverence of the Catacombs, your senses swell and soar as you relive a past long buried beneath the cobblestones you tread.

I wrote this story in the depths of a prairie winter, when all around me the cocoon of swirling snow and icy winds buried everything. Emily Cain believes her life is just such a barren wasteland after her grandmother's death and her fiancé's departure. Bitter, full of resentment, she escapes to Roma — a glorious city in the throes of spring. Years of hearing about the eternal city from her grandmother have made her yearn to be captivated by the past, and yet bitterness prevents her from finding healing and comfort until she lets the lessons of the past teach her a new way to love.

Sometimes it takes the likes of a Coliseum to remind us just how small and insignificant our problems are, and sometimes it takes a glimpse of Michelangelo's Pieta to remind us of how much God loves us.

But one need not visit Rome to see with new eyes. Little boys repeating bedtime prayers, a handmade surprise for an unsuspecting teacher, snow angels pressed in neat rows — my sons did all of these and reminded me anew that God's love heals all, if you let it.

If your heart feels like winter, may I encourage you to take a Roman holiday. Fly away with me to that secret place where our loving Father's arms wrap us in warmth, where the frangipani is sweet, and rest is secure. We can go there anytime, you know. Just by closing our eyes and whispering "Father."

Blessings,
Lois Richer